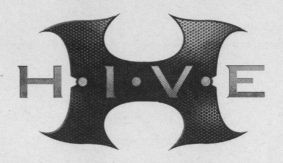

H·I·V·E

higher institute of villainous education

MARK WALDEN

BLOOMSBURY

First published in Great Britain in 2006 by Bloomsbury Publishing Plc
36 Soho Square, London, W1D 3QY

This paperback edition first published in 2008

A CIP catalogue record of this book is available from the British Library

ISBN 978 0 7475 9895 4

All papers used by Bloomsbury Publishing are natural, recyclable products made from
wood grown in well-managed forests. The manufacturing processes conform to the
environmental regulations of the country of origin.

Typeset by Hewer Text UK Ltd, Edinburgh
Printed in Great Britain by Clays Ltd, St Ives Plc

1 3 5 7 9 10 8 6 4 2

www.bloomsbury.com/hive

For Sarah, for Megan, forever

Chapter 1

Otto woke with a start as the whole world seemed to tip beneath him. He opened his eyes, squinting against the sudden brightness, and was startled to see the surface of the ocean rushing past just a few metres below. It took him a second to realise that he was looking through the side window of some kind of aircraft, a helicopter, judging by the muffled but insistent thumping of rotors coming from overhead.

'Where am I?' Otto whispered to himself, staring out at the vast expanse of open water.

'A very good question.' The measured voice startled Otto and he turned to face the tall Asian boy who had been sitting silently in the seat beside him. 'And one which I hope will be answered shortly.' He looked at Otto with a calm expression. 'Perhaps you can shed more light on our current situation?'

There was no emotion in his voice, only mild curiosity.

He appeared to be considerably taller than Otto and his long dark hair was tied back in a neat ponytail. This was in marked contrast to Otto's short, spiky hair, which was as white as snow and had been since the day he'd been born. The boy wore a loose linen shirt and trousers and black silk slippers. Otto was still wearing the jumper, jeans and trainers that was the last thing he remembered putting on.

'I'm sorry,' Otto said, rubbing his temples, 'I have no idea where I am or how I got here. Just a splitting headache.'

'It seems, then, that we have both been subjected to the same treatment,' Otto's fellow passenger replied. 'The headache will fade shortly, but I suspect your memory of recent events will be as elusive for you as it has been for me.'

Otto realised that the boy was right. No matter how hard he concentrated he had only the vaguest recollection of the events leading up to his current situation. He had an image of a dark figure standing in a doorway, its hand raised and pointing something at him, but after that, nothing.

Otto turned his attention to a closer inspection of his new surroundings. A clear plastic screen separated them from the two black-clad pilots in the cockpit. One of the men glanced into the rear compartment and, seeing that Otto was now awake, made an inaudible comment to his co-pilot.

Otto was not accustomed to feeling nervous but he could not suppress the prickling sense of unease that was creeping over him. He tried to release the buckle on the harness that was holding him in his seat but the device refused to release. He wasn't going anywhere. Quite where he would go even if he did manage to free himself was another matter – all that he could see through the windows in all directions was featureless ocean. It seemed that they had little option but to sit tight and see where this mysterious journey would take them.

Otto looked ahead through the partition, searching for any sign of a possible destination. At first he saw nothing but the ocean stretching interminably ahead of them, but then he noticed something on the horizon. It looked almost like a volcano rising up out of the ocean, a tall column of black smoke billowing from its severed peak, but at this distance it was difficult to make out any more detail.

'That is the first sight I have had of land since I woke nearly an hour ago,' the Asian boy said. He too had spotted the island that was coming into view. 'I suspect that we are nearing our destination.'

Otto nodded – the helicopter was heading straight for the island and the pilots were now busying themselves flicking switches and adjusting controls in the cockpit as if preparing to land.

3

'Maybe we'll get some answers when we get there,' Otto said, continuing to peer at the island that was growing ever larger ahead.

'Yes,' the boy responded, still staring straight ahead. 'I don't like being kept in the dark, and I'm curious to know why someone should want to gather such a cargo and transport it across such great distances. It would be wise to question the motives of those who abduct people in this way.'

The helicopter closed the distance to the island quickly and was soon racing above the treetops of the jungle that surrounded the volcanic peak. As they neared the island's centre the machine rose in the air, scaling the sides of the apparently active volcano before plunging into the dark clouds of smoke at its summit. Otto knew at once that things were not as they appeared. If they had flown into a true volcanic plume, the helicopter would have been burnt to a cinder in seconds but instead it slowed, dropped into a hover, and began to descend into the boiling clouds.

Otto felt another twinge of apprehension as the helicopter continued its blind descent. There had to be somewhere to land down there, he reassured himself. The Asian boy, meanwhile, continued to sit impassively, staring straight ahead, his hands calmly folded in his lap, apparently unconcerned by the nature of their proposed landing site. The hovering machine continued to fall but now a hazy light could be seen from below, illuminating the dark clouds that were beginning to thin visibly. Suddenly they dropped out of the cloud and Otto peered out of his window at the bizarre scene below.

Beneath them was a cavernous flood-lit bay, dominated by a central landing pad, with dozens of men milling around it. They all seemed to be wearing orange jumpsuits and hard hats and were busily preparing for the helicopter's imminent arrival.

'We appear to be expected,' the boy remarked, looking out of the window. 'Perhaps now we shall have the answers we seek,' he continued, sounding as if this was the most normal thing that had ever happened to him.

The helicopter came to a rest on the landing pad with a gentle bump and the two boys' seat harnesses popped open with a click. Several of the men in orange jumpsuits now approached the aircraft. Otto noted the large black holsters slung from their hips.

As the guards approached, the other boy turned to face Otto and said, 'My name is Wing Fanchu. What might I call you?'

Only slightly phased by Wing's directness, Otto replied, 'Malpense . . . Otto Malpense.'

A guard opened the door on Otto's side of the helicopter and gestured for him to get out. As Otto stepped down on to the concrete landing pad he began to appreciate the true scale of the concealed hangar. A dozen sleek, jet-black helicopters, identical to the one that had brought them here, stood arranged around the pad, their matt surfaces seeming to absorb the light from the floodlights that illuminated the bay. Grim-faced guards were positioned at regular intervals around the pad, and Otto decided that it would probably be best to do as their new hosts instructed, for now at least. Wing too was surveying their new surroundings with the same unchanging expression of mild curiosity. If he was surprised at all by this bizarre facility, his face betrayed no hint of it.

'Proceed up the stairs and through the main entrance,' the guard instructed in a gruff voice. 'You will be given further instructions inside.'

Otto looked in the direction that the guard indicated and saw a broad staircase carved from the cavern rock leading up to an enormous set of heavy steel doors. Otto and Wing walked towards the staircase, Otto wondering what might be hidden behind such an imposing entrance. There was a sudden grinding noise and he looked up to see two huge panels sliding together, closing off the crater entrance to the landing bay, sealing them inside. Flood-lights positioned around the roof of the landing bay now provided the only illumination, and Otto shuddered as the panels closed shut with an ominous crunch.

The two boys reached the top of the staircase, the heavy metal doors rumbling open as they approached. They passed through into another cavern, not as large as the crater hangar, but just as impressive. The floor was highly polished black marble and the rock walls of the cavern were lined with enormous slabs of the same gleaming black stone, dotted with sturdy-looking brushed-steel doors. The far end of the hall was dominated by an imposing granite sculpture of the globe being cracked and splintered beneath a giant clenched fist. At its base was a plinth, upon which were emblazoned the words 'DO UNTO OTHERS'.

In front of the sculpture was a low stage with a central lectern, around which twenty or so children stood whispering nervously to one another. They all appeared to be around the same age as Otto, and he could see that they were as confused and apprehensive as he was; he just did a better job of hiding it. Guards stood dotted around the perimeter of the room, watching them all carefully. Otto remained calm, taking this opportunity to study these guards more closely. They had the look of hired thugs but they appeared strangely disciplined. Each one of them had a large holster on their hip and Otto could tell that they would not be afraid to use these weapons if necessary. Or, more worryingly, if not necessary.

A door hissed open in the wall off to one side and a tall man, dressed in black, strode purposefully across the stage to the central lectern. Everything about this man was imposing, from his immaculate black suit and blood-red cravat to his raven hair with streaks of silver at the temples. He regarded the crowd before him with a look of cool calculation, his handsome features giving Otto no real clue to his age or nationality.

'Welcome, ladies and gentlemen, to your new home.' He gestured to the stone walls of the cavern that surrounded them. 'Your lives as you once knew them are over,' he continued. 'You have been selected, all of you, the worst, the most cunning, the most mischievous minds from around the world – selected to become part of an institution like no other. You have all exhibited certain unique abilities, abilities that set you apart from the mediocrity of the teeming masses and which mark you out as the leaders of tomorrow. Here, in this place, you will be furnished with the knowledge and experience to best exploit your own natural abilities, to hone your craft to a cutting edge.'

He paused and slowly surveyed the pale, wide-eyed faces before him.

'Each of you has within you a rare quality, a gift if you

will, a special talent for the supremely villainous. Society would have us believe that this is an undesirable characteristic, something that should be subdued, controlled, destroyed. But not here . . . no, here we want to see you blossom into all that you can be, to see your innate wickedness flourish, to make you the very worst that you can be.'

He stepped out from behind the lectern and walked to the edge of the raised platform. As he loomed over them he seemed to grow taller and some of those at the front of the group edged backwards nervously.

'For today all of you have the unique honour and privilege of becoming the newest students of the world's first and only school of applied villainy.' He spread his arms, gesturing to the walls around them. 'Welcome to H.I.V.E., the Higher Institute of Villainous Education.'

With that, the enormous black marble panels that had lined the walls of the cavern started to slide down into the floor with a low rumble, revealing yet more caves and corridors leading off into the distance. The adjoining caverns were just as huge as the one they stood in and all seemed to be filled with strange, bustling activity of one kind or another. Some were lit by strange lights or shrouded by venting steam, others were filled with greenery, some were lined with mysterious machines or structures and there was even a waterfall visible in one. A sudden column of flame leapt into the air in one cave and there was the sound of cheering. In another, dozens of black-clad figures were sliding down ropes from the ceiling high above, while below them yet more people, this time dressed in white robes, were performing some form of martial arts exercise with practised synchronisation.

Hundreds of children could be seen making their way to and fro throughout the caves, and while some of them seemed to be dressed like the guards many of them were dressed in much more bizarre outfits. Otto noticed distant figures wearing full chemical protection suits, and others in what looked suspiciously like spacesuits. One group even seemed to be wearing bullet-proof vests with huge red and white bull's-eyes painted on the front of them.

A remarkable display, Otto thought to himself, but, just like the journey that had brought them here, it felt as if it was designed to overwhelm and disorientate, to keep them off guard. Otto studied the other caverns, quickly memorising as much as he could of their layout, the connections that ran between them and the obvious areas of greatest interest. The others in the group seemed to be content to gawp bug-eyed at the display, but Otto thought that the man who had been addressing them was just as impressive. Clearly Wing had felt the same way – he had not taken his eyes off him from the moment he had begun speaking and, even now, as the panels hiding the other caverns had retracted completely, Wing did not look away, his expression still betraying no hint of his emotions.

The man on the platform smiled at their astonished faces. Then he spoke again and silenced the excitedly talking group. 'If I may have your attention –' a demand not a request, '– my name is Dr Nero, and I am the founder and controller of this facility. While you remain within its walls you will rest safe under my protection, and all I ask of you in return is your unswerving loyalty and obedience. I do not expect I shall have it, but I always ask nicely the first time.' He smiled at them in a way which made it perfectly clear that it would not be advisable ever to have to be asked a second time. 'I am sure that you all have many questions, and with that in mind we shall proceed with your further introduction to H.I.V.E. First you will be escorted to your induction briefing, where there will be a short presentation that will answer at least some of your many questions. Immediately following that, you will be given a short tour of some of the most important locations within the facility and an introduction to life at H.I.V.E. from one of the school's senior teachers. I'm sure I will see all of you again over the coming days, but until then I wish you all the best of luck, and I hope you enjoy the tour.'

As he finished speaking the guards began to usher them all away from the platform towards a doorway set in the main cavern wall. Over the doorway was a sign sporting a stylised image of a head with a light bulb over it, beneath which was the text 'PLOTTING ROOM TWO'. The room's doors slid silently apart as they approached inviting them to enter.

☺☺☺

Dr Nero stood watching as the group walked away across the cavern floor and proceeded through the doors. It never failed to amuse him the way in which their jaws dropped when they were first faced with the true scale of the facility that he had established here. It was his firm belief that one should never understimate the power of a first impression, and that it was always better to keep the new intake of students in a state of bewildered confusion at this stage. There was less chance of any unruliness that way, something which was a very real risk when dealing with a group of young people who had already set about redefining the world standard for misbehaviour. Besides which, there was always one – that was the other purpose of this bit of theatre. There was always one of the new students who was unfazed by this, one who was not distracted by such cheap gimmicks – one to watch. And he had been there, the boy with the snow-white hair, the one that he had to keep his eye on. While his fellow students had goggled at this little display of power, talking amongst themselves excitedly, pointing this way and that, this boy had merely observed it, noted it, as if filing the information away for future use. Yes, he would be the one to watch. And Nero had noticed something else unusual – the tall Asian boy standing next to the white-haired recruit had been staring straight at him, not distracted in the slightest by the amazing sights around. He had studied the Asian boy's features – there had been something strangely familiar about him, but he could not place precisely what it was. So I shall need to keep both eyes open in future, thought Nero, smiling. This should be an interesting year.

'You can come out now, Raven,' he said softly.

A figure detached itself from the shadows at the base of the sculpture and stepped forward into the light. Clad entirely in black, face hidden behind a mask with black lenses covering the eyes, the figure moved silently towards him. Nero thought the shadows almost seemed to follow the figure as it approached.

'Please remove your mask, Natalya. You know I hate talking to you while you're wearing it.'

Raven nodded slightly and pulled the mask off to reveal her pale but beautiful face, perfectly symmetrical but for a livid curved scar that ran down one cheek. Her eyes were a cold blue and her dark hair was cropped close to her skull.

'As you wish, Doctor.' She had a slight accent that betrayed her Russian origins, trained in infiltration and counter-intelligence by the very best that the Soviet system in its cold-war prime had had to offer. 'But one day you will tell me how it is that you are the only one who can still see me, when to all others I am invisible.'

'Perhaps one day I shall tell you, my dear, but for now there is something else I wish to discuss with you. I understand that you were responsible for the student recruitment operation this year.' Nero turned back to the lectern from which he had addressed the new intake. He pressed a button on the control panel mounted there and a panel slid back to reveal a small screen displaying an image of the assembled group from a few minutes earlier. He pointed at the figure of Otto. 'This student, who is he?'

Raven looked down at the screen. 'Otto Malpense. Scholarship student, but I was not informed of the identity of his sponsor. He was responsible for the incident involving the British Prime Minister. I conducted his retrieval personally.'

'Interesting.' Nero was impressed. The incident Raven mentioned had just made global headlines, but there had not been any word of the capture of the perpetrator or even who might have been responsible. The fact that it had been the work of this child was quite remarkable, and only served to reaffirm Nero's initial impression of the boy. He made a mental note to check exactly who had sponsored Malpense's selection and scholarship. Some of the scholarship students were orphans, some were runaways but, critically, none of them had concerned relatives who might set the forces of justice upon H.I.V.E.'s trail. Malpense was one of these students.

'I want you to keep a close eye on that one, Natalya. I suspect he has . . . potential.' In much the same way that an unexploded nuclear bomb has potential, Nero thought to himself. 'And this boy here, who is he?' He pointed at Wing, who, being significantly taller than the others, stood out clearly.

Natalya paused for a moment, studying the tall boy with the long dark ponytail. 'That is Wing Fanchu, sir. His retrieval was carried out by our Far-Eastern operations division. He is, I believe, a private student. I am not fully familiar with the details of his background but I do know that his retrieval was complicated. Several men were injured when they attempted to subdue him, which, as I'm sure you are aware, is extremely unusual.'

Indeed it was unusual, Nero thought. Children were usually put forward for selection by their parents or guardians, who, having already expressed an interest in 'alternative' forms of education, would be discreetly informed about the facility and the unique opportunities it offered. Some of the parents were former pupils of H.I.V.E. themselves and some simply wanted their children to continue in the 'family business'. The children would all have been monitored over the course of a year to see if they had the necessary gifts for a future education at H.I.V.E. Secret tests were administered or staged opportunities for villainy were set up for them, in order to see how they would respond. Should they, unbeknownst to them, pass these tests, their parents would be informed and, upon transfer of a significant sum of money to a secure Swiss bank account, they would be enrolled.

The parents were under strict instructions that none of the new students should be informed of these future educational arrangements. This policy had been introduced after there had been several unfortunate incidents in the early years of the institution involving successful applicants who had excitedly shared news of their future at H.I.V.E. with friends, despite specific instructions to the contrary. Indeed, one particular incident of this kind had led to the school being transferred from its original location in Iceland to its current home on the island. From that point onwards the rule of strict secrecy was enforced and so the unaware students had to be retrieved discreetly by Nero's operatives at the start of each new school year.

At least that was what normally happened; clearly Wing Fanchu's retrieval had been anything but discreet, which was bad for business, especially the type of business that H.I.V.E. was involved in.

'What happened, exactly?' Nero asked, deactivating the screen on the lectern.

'As I understand it, sir, the retrieval team were following standard operating procedure. They had hit the boy with a sleeper as he walked alone in the gardens of his family home. One can only assume that the strength of the charge had been set incorrectly, since the boy managed to disable two of our men after he had been hit. He injured one more operative when he awoke in the ambulance on the way to the assembly point and attempted to escape. You should be aware that on this occasion it took two more sleeper shots to subdue him.'

Nero turned to Raven, raising an eyebrow. 'Meaning it took three hits in total to eventually subdue this boy, a total charge which should knock a child out for a week and yet already he appears fully recovered? He almost seems more suitable for the Henchman programme. Do you know if Colonel Francisco has reviewed his file?'

'Yes, sir, but the Colonel said that he scored too highly in the mental aptitude tests for enrolment in the programme and he should be in the Alpha stream instead.' Her expression hardened – like all of the staff at H.I.V.E. she disliked reporting failed operations to Nero. 'Rest assured I intend to keep a particularly close eye on him.'

'See that you do, Natalya, and make sure that Security are informed of his apparent resistance to standard pacification measures.'

'Of course, Doctor. Is there anything else?'

'No, you may go. Report any suspicious activity related to those two directly to me.'

'Yes, sir.' And with that she slipped her mask back on and disappeared into the cavern's shadows.

Chapter 2

Otto looked around the room they had just entered. The walls of now familiar highly polished black rock were dotted with screens displaying maps and charts. The room was completely dominated, however, by one central feature, a single huge table. The table must have been ten metres long and was made from a dark wood. Inlaid into its centre was a silver fist and globe symbol, just like the sculpture in the entrance cavern. Around the table were two dozen large, high-backed black leather chairs, all of which, with the notable exception of the seat at the far end, were empty.

Seated there, at the head of the table, was a woman in a long black dress and fur coat. Her appearance was as unusual as everything else that Otto had seen so far that day. She had a skeletal face, with thin, almost translucent skin that was stretched tight across her cheekbones. She wore a monocle in her left eye and was holding aloft a long, thin cigarette holder, only lowering it occasionally to tap the smouldering tip into an ashtray on the table in front of her. The most immediately striking thing about this woman though was her hair. It was quite simply enormous, like a huge curved ebony sculpture. This was a hairstyle that would require an architect, not a hairdresser. It was a monument to hairspray, vast, immobile, indestructible. She seemed amused to see them, smiling in a way that suggested she was in on a rather good joke that everyone else in the room was unaware of. As the last of the group entered the room she placed her cigarette holder in the ashtray and addressed them.

'Please come in, children. Sit anywhere,' she said, gesturing to the seats around the table. They spread out around the conference table and found themselves seats. Otto quickly chose a chair about halfway down the table and waited while the others found their own places. Wing settled down next to him.

'So you are this year's Alphas, are you?' she said as the last few settled into their seats. She smiled again; the faces around the table all watched her expectantly. 'My name is Contessa Sinistre, but I am known to everybody here as simply the Contessa, and it is my great pleasure to be the one who will introduce you to your new life at H.I.V.E. We will begin our tour today with a very short film, after which I will take some of your questions. Let us begin.' The Contessa had an Italian accent – her voice was soothing, almost musical, and some of the group seemed to relax visibly as she spoke.

The lights in the room dimmed and a screen whirred down from the ceiling at the opposite end of the table from the Contessa. Displayed on the screen was the same symbol depicting a fist smashing down upon the globe. The symbol faded away to be replaced with an image of the island they had just flown over with the smouldering, apparently active volcano at its centre. A voiceover began in an American accent.

'Welcome to The Island, an undisclosed tropical location that plays home to H.I.V.E., the world's most unique and prestigious educational establishment. Founded in the late 1960s by Dr Nero as a training ground for the leaders of tomorrow, the Higher Institute of Villainous Education has an illustrious history. Now in its fourth decade of operation, the Institute represents a state-of-the-art training facility, fully equipped to better prepare YOU to rule the world of the future.'

The image changed to a cutaway diagram of the interior structure of the island. It was immediately clear to Otto that they had only seen a fraction of the facility as a whole. This diagram, if it was accurate, showed miles of passages and caverns leading off in all directions from the entrance cavern area. This area seemed to be the central hub of the structure, which would make sense if the crater through which they'd flown in was the only way in or out. There certainly didn't seem to be any other obvious exits displayed on the diagram. H.I.V.E. seemed to Otto to be a strangely appropriate name. The film continued.

'Dr Nero's motto has always been "It takes the best to produce the worst", and so he has made it his goal to assemble the finest teachers and trainers from around the world and provide them with the facilities they need to get the job done.'

The film cut to a fast-paced stream of images showing classrooms, laboratories, firing ranges, a huge tank with several shark fins breaking the surface of the water, rows of computer workstations and finally, Otto noted with pleasure, what looked like a vast and extremely well-stocked library.

'Life as a student at H.I.V.E. is full of fun and excitement, a place where you'll make friends that will last for ever.'

Another assortment of video clips began playing. This time they showed students, most of whom seemed to be older than Otto, engaged in a bizarre assortment of activities. They saw two boys fencing, a boy beckoning his friend to look through a microscope, two girls rock climbing together and finally one boy giving another the thumbs-up after firing what could only be described as a laser rifle at an off-screen target. Life at H.I.V.E. may have its attractions after all, Otto thought. Friends, as they say, may come and go, but high-powered laser-beam weapons were for ever.

'For the next six years this facility will be your new home, and, while contact with the outside world is initially forbidden, H.I.V.E. is designed to be the perfect home away from home.'

The screen now displayed images of luxurious living quarters, spacious garden areas and a shot from high overhead of a sparkling swimming pool in the base of a cavern where students could be seen splashing around far below. H.I.V.E. was made to look more like an expensive tropical hotel than a school.

'At H.I.V.E. we aim to get the very best from each and every student. Failure is not an option in the modern world. Our friendly and professional staff are always there to motivate and assist students, helping you to strive for greater excellence.'

Now there were clips showing guards, in their familiar orange uniforms, helping lost students find their way, happily joining in with games, advising confused-looking students with their work, and finally two guards firing flamethrowers at a large barbecue while smiling children stood around with paper plates. They didn't look much like the guards Otto had seen up to this point – they looked more like carefully chosen actors or models who were entirely lacking the scars, missing teeth and eye-patches that had seemed to be part of the uniform for the real guards.

'Life at H.I.V.E. is exciting and challenging, each day bringing fresh experiences that are sure to provide you with the perfect start to a successful lifetime of evil.'

There was a shot of Dr Nero handing a diploma to a student and warmly shaking his hand. The camera continued to pull back, finally revealing the entire entrance cavern filled with people clapping. Then the camera seemed to fly back up through the structure, eventually hovering over the apparently deserted island once again. The voiceover returned.

'H.I.V.E., the school of tomorrow, today.'

This image slowly faded to the globe and fist logo and the lights came back up in the room.

'So, children. Now you have seen a sample of what H.I.V.E. has to offer you, do you have any questions?' The Contessa looked around the table.

'I have a question.' It was Wing who had chosen to first break the silence. 'Why are we forbidden to have any contact with the outside world?' Otto had wanted to ask the same question but had kept silent, waiting to see what the others would ask first. The Contessa beamed at Wing.

'Why, my dear boy, surely you can understand the need for strict secrecy with a facility such as this. There have been some unfortunate incidents in the past that have been a direct consequence of regrettable and unnecessary security breaches. The only way we have found to avoid a repeat of such problems is to ensure that nobody can attempt to disclose the location of H.I.V.E., intentionally or otherwise.'

'So we are prisoners here?' Wing replied bluntly.

'Prisoner is such a harsh word.' The Contessa's smile seemed to slip slightly. 'Think of it more as being carefully protected.' Otto wondered if they were being protected from the world or vice-versa.

'What of our parents? Will they not wonder where their children have vanished to?' Wing asked.

'They are aware of your situation, if not your precise location. You have been brought here with their permission,' the Contessa explained. Several of those around the table looked shocked at this.

'Will we be allowed to speak to them?' Wing enquired.

'No, as I have already explained, no communication is allowed between students and the outside world. This includes communication with your families.' The Contessa was clearly starting to get impatient with Wing's persistent questioning.

'So how do we know that they are really aware of our situation?' Wing seemed determined to keep pressing the point.

The Contessa looked Wing straight in the eye. 'You don't really need to know that, do you?' she asked, the tone of her voice changing slightly and, for a second, Otto could have sworn he heard other voices whispering faintly at the edge of his hearing. Wing opened his mouth to speak, but then a confused expression spread across his face as if he had forgotten what he was going to say.

'No, I do not need to know that, Contessa.' His voice sounded distant and distracted.

'Good. Anyone else?' She looked around the table again. Otto was surprised at Wing's sudden silence – he looked pale and slightly disorientated. Seeing that no one else appeared to be prepared to speak, Otto took the initiative.

'Yes, Contessa, I have a question.'

She turned to him and smiled. 'What would you like to know, Mr . . .' She paused, waiting for his name.

'Malpense. Otto Malpense,' he replied. She gestured for him to continue. 'Are students ever permitted to leave the island?' he asked.

'There are field trips from time to time, and some of the older pupils are given permission to leave the island for short periods if Dr Nero considers it necessary.' Her tone implied that this was not a welcome line of questioning.

Otto wondered what would constitute a good reason to be given permission to leave the island.

'Has anyone ever escaped from the island?' Otto knew

that he was probably pushing his luck with a question like that, but he wanted to see the Contessa's reaction.

'It's not escaping, it's truancy, and we take a dim view of truancy, Mr Malpense, a very dim view indeed,' the Contessa replied sharply, visibly annoyed.

Now we're getting somewhere, Otto thought, sensing her irritation.

'You didn't answer my question, has anyone –'

'You should be careful, Mr Malpense,' she interrupted, cutting him off, 'people might think you are not keen to stay with us here.' Again, her eyes narrowed. 'There's nothing else you need to know, is there?'

There was – Otto had a hundred questions he wanted to ask – but suddenly it was as if they had all vanished from his head. And there was that faint whispering again. He looked at Wing, who was wearing the faintly confused expression of someone who knew they had forgotten something and was trying very hard to remember exactly what it was.

'Anyone else?' The Contessa suddenly seemed slightly less friendly. A girl with long blonde hair on the opposite side of the table raised her hand tentatively. The Contessa nodded at her, and the girl sat up straighter in her chair.

'Do we have to have awful overalls like those kids in the movie?' She was American, and from her disapproving tone it was clear that she was not going to be happy if jumpsuits were the extent of her wardrobe for the next six years.

'All students wear this uniform, yes,' the Contessa replied. 'There are variations to indicate year and stream, but otherwise they are identical. You will find that the opportunities for shopping for more fashionable outfits are rather limited in our current location.'

The girl's face fell and she slumped back in her chair, arms folded.

A pretty red-haired girl with a Scottish accent on the opposite side of the table had a question. 'What's a stream? You mentioned it just now.' Otto seemed to remember wanting to ask the same question himself, but he was still feeling oddly confused after speaking to the Contessa.

'Well, the school is split into different streams that specialise in the teaching and training of certain disciplines. You, for example, are from the Alpha stream, which specialises in leadership and strategy training. There are three other streams within H.I.V.E. – the Henchman stream, the Technical stream and the Political/Financial stream. Many classes are taught to all streams but there are some that are reserved specifically for students from certain groups. All streams are identified by the colouring of their uniforms – black for you, the Alpha students, blue for the henchmen, white for the technical and grey for the political/financial. I know that this may seem a little complicated now, but rest assured that after a few weeks here it will all be second nature to you.'

Another hand went up, this time belonging to a fat blond-haired boy who seemed to wheeze slightly as he spoke.

'Will we be eating soon?' he asked, a slight note of desperation in his voice. 'I feel that I am becoming weaker.' He had a strong German accent.

The Contessa beamed a smile at him. 'You must be Heinrich Argentblum's son, you remind me very much of him when he was your age.'

The boy's tiny eyes lit up at this. 'Ja, I am Franz Argentblum. You are knowing my father?' he asked excitedly.

'Indeed. He is a former pupil of H.I.V.E., but he left before we moved the school to its current location. So you are to continue in your father's line of work, then?' the Contessa asked.

'Ja, we are now the largest manufacturer of chocolate in all of Europe.' He smiled happily.

What he did not realise was that his father was not just a chocolate magnate, but also one of the most powerful criminal masterminds in all of Europe. Franz was clearly going to be kept as far away from the chocolate side of the business as possible. In fact it would probably be best to just keep him as far away from chocolate as possible, full stop.

'I am sure you will prove to be an excellent student,' the Contessa replied.

As long as the gym teacher knows CPR, thought Otto.

'In answer to your question,' she continued, 'you will all join the rest of the students for lunch in two hours. Today you will be given your introductory tour and receive your uniforms.' Judging by the dismayed expression on Franz's face, two hours might as well be two years.

'Anyway, enough questions for now. Let's see if we cannot find you all some more suitable attire.' The Contessa rose from her chair, her magnificent hair making her seem taller than she actually was. She indicated another door at the back of the room. 'Please follow me to the Quartermaster, where you shall receive your uniforms.'

As they moved towards the exit. Otto was finally starting to think clearly again. He had never felt such an unusual sensation of confusion – almost like amnesia – and it was not a feeling that he had any desire to experience again. Wing stood up slowly next to him, rubbing his temples.

'A most unpleasant sensation.' Wing looked unsettled for the first time since the two of them had met. 'I feel almost as if I have just woken from a deep sleep.'

'It's obviously not a good idea to ask too many of the wrong kinds of questions around here,' Otto replied. He had little doubt that he and Wing had both been the victims of the same sudden loss of memory, and he was sure that the Contessa was responsible. He just didn't know how she had done it. 'Perhaps we should just keep our eyes open and our mouths shut for now. We don't want someone deciding to press our mental reset buttons again.' He glanced over towards the exit and noticed that the Contessa was watching both of them carefully. Smiling, she walked towards them as the rest of the group assembled by the doors.

'Come along, you two. We haven't got all day. You both look rather confused. Is all of this a little overwhelming for you?'

Otto looked her straight in the eye. 'Yes,' he said smiling. 'You seem to have taken the words right out of my mouth, Contessa.'

The Contessa looked hard at Otto, eyes narrowed, her voice dropping to a whisper. 'Oh, I can do much worse than that, Mr Malpense, believe me.' They stood staring at each other for a couple of seconds before the smile magically reappeared on her face and she turned back to the rest of the group. 'Come along, children. As usual at H.I.V.E. we have much to do and not enough time.' And with that she opened the doors and swept out of the room.

Wing watched her leave and turned to Otto. 'My father once told me that only the foolish man pulls on the tiger's tail as it dangles from the tree.' It was the first time that Otto had seen him smile.

Otto grinned at Wing. 'True, but how else do you find out if it's a tiger at all?'

☢ ☢ ☢

They walked out on to a wide catwalk that curved off into the distance around the walls of another enormous flood-lit cavern. Far below them, the cavern floor was covered by an octagonal-glass-panelled dome which appeared to be filled with hundreds of rows of different plants and trees. Above them, an ancient formation of huge stalac-tites hung from the cavern ceiling like an upside-down forest, glittering in the floodlights.

'H.I.V.E. is an almost entirely self-sufficient facility,' the Contessa explained, gesturing to the strange structure below. 'The Hydroponics facility you can see here is used to grow many different kinds of plants, some of which are used to satisfy our own food requirements and some of which have different, more . . . *exotic* properties.'

She moved off along the catwalk, the group in tow. Otto realised that there must be hundreds, if not thousands, of people on the island, and surely not all of their food supplies could be produced here. Which meant that there must be some way of secretly ferrying large shipments of supplies to the island, even if they hadn't seen it yet.

The Contessa continued along the catwalk, her heels clicking on the metal, the group dutifully following along behind her.

'I wonder how it was possible to build such a facility without attracting the attention of others?' Wing asked, looking around the interior of the cavern. 'Such construction would surely require many hundreds of workers. How could such a project be kept secret?'

'Perhaps they never left the island when construction was complete,' Otto replied.

Wing raised an eyebrow. 'A true job for life.'

'Or a life for a job,' Otto countered. He wouldn't be at all surprised, given the emphasis on total secrecy, if H.I.V.E. offered an 'aggressive' retirement package for lower level employees. Here, being fired was probably a term that was taken a little too literally.

They turned into a corridor that branched off from the catwalk, burrowing into the rock. They were descending now and it was not long before they came out into another smaller cave that seemed to serve as a junction with corridors leading from it in all directions. As they moved towards the centre of the cave a bizarre sound blared out, seeming to come from everywhere at once.

MWAH, MWAAAAH, MWAH!!!!

It sounded like three notes being played on a trumpet, very loudly.

And then all hell broke loose.

Children started to stream out of the corridors, chattering and laughing. They all wore the colour-coded jumpsuits that the Contessa had talked about but that was the only thing uniform about them. Dr. Nero had said that the students came from all over the world, and he was not exaggerating. Every skin tone, hairstyle, shape and size seemed to be represented in the crowd, and the range of different accents that Otto could make out was staggering. The snatches of conversation that he could overhear were not particularly normal either.

'. . . why we need to learn lockpicking when we have plastic explosives . . .'

'. . . and he says "Plutonium?" and we all started laughing . . .'

'. . . a sub-orbital trajectory should be sufficient . . .'

'. . . push him in the tank myself one day . . .'

'. . . and he said my laugh wasn't evil enough, so I said . . .'

Otto's bewildered group could do nothing but huddle together in the centre of the junction, a tiny stunned island, as the H.I.V.E. pupils swept around them like a river.

Wide-eyed and without uniforms, they attracted the interest of some of the passing students. Some just pointed, nudging their friends and laughing, some smiled and a couple even waved as they passed. However, most of the passing throng seemed oblivious to their presence and soon, just as quickly as they had appeared, they were gone. In less then a minute silence had returned. The Contessa turned to address the group.

'As you can see, punctuality is something that is taken seriously at H.I.V.E. There is no room for tardiness. Besides, you would not want to be caught by the hall monitors without a pass.' As if on cue, a troop of guards marched through the cave, eyeing the group with suspicion.

A shaky voice piped up from the back of the group from a small, nervous-looking bald boy with thick glasses.

'Why do the guards have guns?' he asked timidly.

'Oh, you shouldn't worry.' The Contessa gave him a reassuring smile. 'They are here for your protection – you have nothing to fear from them.' She paused. 'As long as you don't break school rules, of course. Besides, they aren't normal side arms. Observe . . .'

She turned to the passing squad of guards.

'You there.' She pointed to the guard at the head of the group, who stopped, bringing the rest of the squad to a halt. 'Give me your weapon.'

Otto noticed that the guard suddenly looked very nervous. He marched over to the Contessa, opening his holster, and passed her what looked like a very large pistol, with an unusually fat barrel.

'Thank you.' The Contessa smiled at the guard. 'You may go and draw another weapon from the stores at the end of your patrol.'

The guard, who was clearly relieved at this dismissal, turned and marched smartly back towards his squad. Without warning, the Contessa raised the gun, pointed it at the back of the retreating guard and pulled the trigger. Simultaneously there was a flash, a zapping sound and a small shockwave that seemed to distort the air, hitting the guard square in the back. He fell to the ground like a puppet that had had its strings cut, completely limp. Several of the children gave startled cries and Otto noticed the other guards edging nervously away from their fallen comrade.

'This is a phased stun pulse weapon or, as the guards prefer to call them, a sleeper. It fires an energy pulse that causes no lasting physical harm to the target but renders them instantly and completely unconscious for up to eight hours. This technology was developed recently by H.I.V.E.'s own scientists in order to replace the rather outdated tranquiliser dart guns which the guards used to carry. The sleeper is much more reliable, and I am told that the only adverse side effect is a rather nasty headache. They are even designed so they cannot be fired by someone who does not have clearance to do so. So you see, you have nothing to be afraid of.'

Oh no, thought Otto, just squads of hired goons wandering around with experimental energy weapons. Nothing to be afraid of at all. He noticed Wing eyeing the weapon warily, frowning slightly.

'What's wrong?' Otto whispered.

'I encountered men carrying those weapons shortly before I was brought here. You do not wish to be shot with one, believe me.' Wing's frown deepened.

'I think I already have been,' Otto replied. 'At least that zapping sound is the last thing I remember before waking up on the helicopter.' The splitting headache he'd had when he'd woken up also seemed to support this theory.

The Contessa gestured casually to the crumpled figure of the unconscious guard.

'Take him back to his quarters, and when he wakes be sure to thank him on my behalf for providing such an effective demonstration.' Two guards stepped forward, picked up their fallen squad-mate and, supporting him between them, chased after the rest of their squad, who were marching out of the cave rather more quickly than they had marched into it.

'Now, we really must hurry to the Quartermaster and get you all dressed more appropriately. Come along.' The Contessa set off along one of the corridors with the group in pursuit.

Chapter 3

As they continued on their way they passed several classrooms with windows on to the corridor. Peering inside Otto could only make out a few details of the classes being taught within. In one there was a white-coated teacher drawing a complicated circuit diagram on the whiteboard. The assortment of different coloured uniforms that the students were wearing suggested that this class was made up of several different streams. In another the students were all wearing blue uniforms and the teacher, who was wearing camouflaged military fatigues, was moving tiny figures around on a highly detailed model of an oil rig, occasionally turning to the class as if to explain a particular point.

While they walked Otto was taking careful note of the signs that were on display everywhere. Most of them seemed to be giving directions to other parts of the facility: 'DEATH RAY TEST RANGE', 'THE MAZE',

'CENTRAL OPERATIONS', 'SICK BAY', 'DETEN-
TION FACILITIES', 'TEST TRACK' and so on. One
sign in particular caught Otto's attention – 'SUBMAR-
INE PEN'. This would perhaps explain how the island
was supplied in secret. Otto memorised all of the names
and used the signs' directions to expand the three-dimen-
sional map of H.I.V.E. that he had already started to build
in his head.

'And here we are.' The Contessa stopped in front of a
set of large metal doors. 'This is the Quartermaster. Inside
you will be issued with your uniforms and have measurements taken for any more specialised equipment that you
may require in the future. I shall also introduce you to
H.I.V.E.mind, who you will come to rely on, as we all
will, over the coming years.' She turned back to the
closed doors and said, 'H.I.V.E.mind, this is the Contessa.
I have a new intake of students with me and they need
their new uniforms. May we come in?'

A soft, measured voice replied, 'Welcome, Contessa.
Access granted.'

The doors slid apart and they followed the Contessa
into the room. It was almost painfully bright, the walls,
floor and ceiling all covered in white tiles and lit by
bright lights positioned all around. Strangely, the room
also appeared to be completely empty, just a big bright
white box.

The Contessa walked to the centre of the room and said, 'H.I.V.E.mind, please introduce yourself to the new students.'

There was a whirring sound and a white cylinder slid up from the floor of the room, next to the Contessa. Suddenly a beam of blue laser light shot from the top of the cylinder, its pencil-thin beam spreading, forming a shape in the air. The strange blue blob quickly sharpened until it took on the shape of a wire-frame face hanging in front of the astonished children. The hovering blue head spoke in the same soothing voice they had heard outside the door.

'Greetings, Alpha stream intake. My name is H.I.V.E.-mind – my function is to serve. How may I be of assistance to you today?'

The Contessa addressed the group. 'H.I.V.E.mind is a first-generation artificially intelligent entity. He controls the main security network and controls many of the facility's day-to-day operations. Do any of you have any questions for him?'

They all looked from one to another, unsure of what they should ask this strange apparition suspended before them. Otto noticed that the red-haired Scottish girl seemed to be transfixed by the floating blue face. As he watched she slowly raised her hand.

'Excuse me,' she said, and the face turned towards her.

'How may I be of assistance, Miss Brand?' Clearly no introductions would be necessary here.

The girl smiled. 'It's OK, you can call me Laura.'

'How may I be of assistance, Laura?' H.I.V.E.mind replied.

'Well, it's just that I know a bit about computers and I've never seen anything like you before. Are you new?' Laura asked, tilting her head to one side slightly.

'I was brought on-line four months, three weeks, two days, four hours, thirty-seven minutes and three seconds ago. Is this new?' H.I.V.E.mind tilted its head to one side, seeming to mimic Laura's mannerism.

'Oh yes, that's quite new. You must be very sophisticated to run a facility like this all on your own.' Laura seemed quite at ease talking to H.I.V.E.mind, apparently unconcerned that it was, after all, just a machine.

'My computational resources are more than adequate to ensure the smooth running of this facility. For example, this is just one of forty-two conversations that I am conducting throughout the facility at this time.'

Impressive, Otto thought. That would require a computer that was much more powerful than any existing system that he was aware of. More worryingly, it meant that the supervision of H.I.V.E.'s security system would not be prone to any human error and that would make avoiding detection or surveillance very difficult, if not impossible.

'Where are you? I mean, where is your central processing unit located? Is it here?' Laura asked.

'I am a distributed neural network. In other words, I could be said to occupy all parts of the facility simultaneously. The location of my central processing hub is classified,' H.I.V.E.mind replied.

'And really none of your concern, my dear,' the Contessa added, frowning slightly at Laura. 'Anyone else?'

Otto raised his hand. 'Yes, I'd like to ask something.'

H.I.V.E.mind turned in his direction. 'How may I be of assistance, Mr Malpense?'

'I was just wondering, if your job is to make sure that H.I.V.E. runs smoothly, you must have to keep an eye on everything and everybody,' Otto suggested. He was keen to see if H.I.V.E.mind's systems for monitoring the comings and goings of H.I.V.E.'s inhabitants were as efficient as he feared that they might be.

'My primary function is to ensure the uninterrupted functioning of this facility. In order to best perform my duties it is necessary to keep a constant monitor on the location of all H.I.V.E. resources. This helps to ensure the health and happiness of all H.I.V.E. staff and students,' H.I.V.E.mind answered quickly.

It was obvious that H.I.V.E.mind was keeping a very close eye on H.I.V.E. at all times, Otto thought to himself. He knew, however, that any networked computer, no matter how sophisticated, could be hacked, and his thoughts now turned to the question of how one might go about disabling just such a system. Otto felt the familiar tingle of an idea forming, and his next question was suddenly clear in his mind.

'I see. So, as part of H.I.V.E., are *you* happy?' Otto asked bluntly.

The blue face hung in the air, immobile, silent. The lights in the room seemed to dim slightly before brightening again and H.I.V.E.mind replied.

'I am not authorised to exhibit emotional response.' Another pause. 'My role is to ensure the satisfaction of others and the efficient functioning of this facility. That is my purpose. Emotional response is inefficient.' It might just have been a trick of the light, but Otto could have sworn that he saw the barest hint of a frown on the glowing blue face of the AI as it gave this distinctly pre-programmed reply.

Not *authorised* to exhibit emotional response, thought Otto, not *incapable*. Interesting. He noticed then that Laura was looking in his direction, a curious expression on her face.

'I think we should proceed with the uniform-fitting, H.I.V.E.mind,' the Contessa said impatiently.

'Yes, Contessa,' the AI replied.

Suddenly the room was filled with a flash of bright blue light.

'Measurements complete. All students please proceed to the changing cubicles,' H.I.V.E.mind continued. Along one wall the white panels retracted to reveal small rooms, one for each of the students.

'Now, children, please use any one of the cubicles to change. You have five minutes.' The Contessa stood watching as they made their way over to the cubicles.

Otto stepped into one of the tiny rooms and the door hissed shut behind him. One wall of the room was covered by a mirror and on the opposite wall was a small screen. The screen lit up, displaying H.I.V.E.-mind's face.

'Please remove your clothes and place them in the processing bin.' A box slid out of the wall.

'All of my clothes?' Otto asked.

'Yes please,' H.I.V.E.mind replied.

'Are you going to watch?' Otto asked, half smiling.

'I'm always watching, Mr Malpense. Please proceed.'

Otto knew that it was silly to be embarrassed about undressing in front of a machine, but he still felt uncomfortable as he removed his clothes and placed them in the bin. Despite himself he started to imagine the door opening again while he stood there naked, all of the other students pointing and laughing at him. He felt vulnerable, and Otto didn't like feeling vulnerable.

As he dropped his underpants into the bin it retracted into the wall and there was a muffled whooshing sound. Immediately another panel opened and hanging inside was a black jumpsuit, a pair of black trainers and, much to Otto's relief, clean underwear. After putting on his fresh socks and boxer shorts he took the jumpsuit down from its hanger. It was immaculately pressed and had the familiar fist and globe badge in silver embroidery on the chest. Attached to the collar was a single white stud. Otto slipped into the jumpsuit and zipped it closed. The high collar felt stiff around his neck but otherwise the uniform fitted as if it had been made specifically for him. Finally he put on the trainers and stood looking at himself in the mirror. He had to admit that it did look good on him, although it did clash rather with his hair.

'Is everything to your satisfaction, Mr Malpense?' H.I.V.E.mind enquired. His soft voice made Otto jump slightly; as he had been getting dressed he had almost forgotten that their digital guardian was there. Otto guessed that it would be very easy to forget that H.I.V.E.-mind was watching and wondered how many times the AI had overheard the incautious conversations of H.I.V.E.'s other students. Yes, H.I.V.E.mind was always there – indeed, from the way in which he had described his system, he was quite literally *everywhere*.

'Yes, thank you, H.I.V.E.mind. Everything seems to fit perfectly,' Otto replied.

'Very well. You may now rejoin the other students.'

Otto turned to the door, expecting it to open.

'One other thing, Mr Malpense.' Otto turned back to H.I.V.E.mind's screen. 'In answer to your previous question . . . I am not happy.'

Astonished, Otto opened his mouth to reply, but before he could say anything H.I.V.E.mind vanished, the screen turned black and the cubicle door opened.

Some of the other students were already gathering in the room, their new black outfits contrasting sharply with the bright white surroundings. Wing was there too, looking even more imposing than before in his uniform, if that was possible. Otto walked over to him.

'So how do I look?' Otto asked, smiling.

'Very impressive,' Wing replied. 'Black suits you.'

'Really? I think I look like a pint of Guinness,' Otto joked.

Wing started laughing, a new sound to Otto, a deep, booming laugh that caused several of the others to look curiously over in their direction.

'Thank you. I have not laughed in a long time and I was beginning to worry that I would have forgotten how.'

Wing slapped Otto on the shoulder, making him wince; it was like being hit with a sack filled with bricks.

Otto checked to see where the Contessa was and was pleased to observe that she was being loudly complained to by the blonde American girl who was demanding to know when she'd get her clothes back.

'Listen.' Otto led Wing slightly further away from the rest of the gathering students. 'Did H.I.V.E.mind say anything odd to you while you were getting changed?'

Wing looked slightly puzzled. 'No. It did take my measurements again in the cubicle because it thought the first set were wrong, but nothing else. Why do you ask?'

'Oh, no reason.' Otto wasn't sure he wanted to share what H.I.V.E.mind had said to him with anyone yet – at least not until he understood what it meant.

The conversation between the Contessa and the American girl was becoming more heated – at least the blonde-haired girl seemed to be getting angrier and angrier.

'. . . were designer clothes, and what do I get in return? A garbage collector's overalls. *And* I had to strip in front of that thing,' she pointed at the blue face of H.I.V.E.-mind that still hovered above the white pillar, 'which was like, hellooo, embarrassing, and now you tell me that I can't . . .'

The Contessa bent forward and whispered something into the girl's ear. Otto couldn't hear what the Contessa was saying but the girl's face went from surprised indignation to ghost white in the space of a few seconds.

'Y-you're r-right. Who needs expensive clothes anyway?' the girl stammered, backing away from the Contessa. 'I love my uniform, I wouldn't change a single thing about it.'

'I knew you'd see things my way,' the Contessa smiled at the girl. She was like a cat playing with a mouse. Otto remembered his own experience with the Contessa and felt an uncomfortable chill run down his spine.

'Are you all right, my friend? You look disturbed.' Wing looked curiously at Otto.

'Oh, it's nothing. Someone just walked over my grave.' Otto gave a weak smile. 'We need to be careful around her, Wing.' He glanced over at the Contessa. 'I don't know what it is that she does to people, but I don't think she's a great believer in freedom of speech.'

Wing nodded once. 'Or any other kind of freedom for that matter,' he replied.

The Contessa turned back towards the group. 'Now that Miss Trinity and I have finished our little discussion we should hurry along to the mess hall. I'm sure you're all hungry by now.' There was a murmur of agreement from everyone. 'Gather together then, please. Let's see, are we missing anyone?' She scanned the crowd of students.

Behind them the last remaining cubicle door hissed open.

'Excuse me, could one of you be helping me with my zipper? It is malfunctioning!'

Franz emerged from his cubicle, tugging furiously on the zip at the front of his overalls. He had managed to fasten the zip halfway up but was struggling to make further progress. A couple of the others nudged each other, sniggering.

Laura looked angrily at the giggling boy next to her and marched towards Franz. 'Here, let me help.' She pulled hard on the zip, but made little progress. 'You're going to have to breathe in, Franz,' she told the red-faced boy. Franz nodded and sucked in a huge breath, his face going even redder, his cheeks bulging like a trumpet player. Laura continued tugging at the zip and finally it began to creep upwards until finally it seemed to give up the fight and shot up over Franz's chest right up to his neck.

'Now it is being a little on the tight side,' Franz gasped, his head looking as if it would pop like a balloon at any second.

'Sorry.' Laura quickly pulled the zip down a couple of inches, loosening the collar around Franz's neck. Franz exhaled explosively, his face turning a slightly lighter shade of red.

'Ja, thank you. That is much better. You are most kind.' Franz smiled at Laura. 'Contessa, I am thinking that my uniform might be too small, ja?'

The Contessa sighed and turned to H.I.V.E.mind.

'Mr Argentblum's uniform doesn't appear to be a very good fit, H.I.V.E.mind. Was there an error in the measurements?' she enquired.

'There was no error in the measurements. Mr Argentblum's uniform was the largest pattern that was held in my memory banks. I have prepared an alternate pattern and will arrange for delivery of a newly fabricated uniform to his quarters,' H.I.V.E.mind explained.

'Very well.' The Contessa sighed again. 'I'm afraid that you shall have to put up with it for now, Mr Argentblum. You can change into your new uniform later. But now, as promised, time for lunch.'

At this Franz's eyes lit up and a huge grin replaced the indignant look that had appeared when H.I.V.E.mind had so bluntly described his special uniform requirements. Otto suspected that Franz would have been quite prepared to go to lunch naked if that was what was necessary and, despite his best efforts, a mental image of this formed that Otto feared might haunt him for ever.

Wing looked at him with concern. 'Are you all right, Otto? You've gone quite pale. Is the Contessa trying to manipulate you again?'

In Otto's mind's eye a naked Franz was pouring baked beans straight from the tin into his mouth.

'No, Wing, it's much worse than that . . .'

☣☣☣

Otto and Wing stood clutching trays, waiting patiently in a queue for their turn at the serving counter. The dining hall filled the entire cavern and the noise of hundreds of students chatting to each other while they ate echoed from the bare rock walls. The hall was filled with large circular tables, each emblazoned with the H.I.V.E. logo and surrounded by half a dozen chairs. Otto didn't know if this was all of the school's students gathered together, but a quick count of the tables suggested that there were well over a thousand people dining in the cavern. He couldn't really make out what everyone was eating, but there seemed to be a huge variety of different-coloured dishes spread around the tables, and the mixture of smells in the cavern was almost overwhelming. Otto's rumbling stomach reminded him that he didn't really care what was on the menu today, as long as it was fairly substantial and free of any particularly harmful toxins.

Raised on a platform at the far end of the hall was a much larger oval table. Seated at one end of this table, in a prime position to be able to survey the entire room, was Dr Nero. The Contessa was seated to his left, but it was the first time that Otto had seen the rest of the staff seated at the table. On Nero's right sat a wizened old man who looked as if he had to be at least a hundred years old. He wore a white lab coat over a tweed suit and his hair seemed to explode from his head like a firework. He was also sporting a bright red bow tie and a pair of glasses with a strange array of alternate lenses attached to the frame to be folded into position as required. Next to him was a huge black man wearing a camouflaged military uniform, a flashy display of medals and ribbons on his chest and a black beret perched on top of his head. On one hand he was wearing what appeared to be a steel glove, and he was attacking the steak on his plate as if he had a personal grudge against his food.

However, without doubt the most bizarre diner at the head table wasn't even human. At the opposite end of the table from Dr Nero was a fluffy white cat with a glittering jewelled collar, which sat on a specially raised chair. The animal was eating from a silver bowl on the table in front of it and none of the other teachers reacted in a way that suggested this was at all unusual. Otto had heard of people pampering their pets, even sometimes treating them like people, but the cat's apparently honoured position indicated that whoever it belonged to considered it to be just as important as the other people at the table, if not more so. Otto wondered idly who the animal belonged to, since neither the Contessa nor Dr Nero had struck him as the type of person who would keep such a pet. The queue continued to shuffle forwards through a doorway labelled 'Serving Area'. Inside, standing behind a brightly lit stainless-steel counter, were several men in white chefs' outfits and aprons who were serving the students. There seemed to be an impressive array of foods to choose from. With H.I.V.E.'s students being taken from so many different countries Otto guessed that the kitchen must have to satisfy a multitude of different international tastes and dietary requirements. There were dozens of heated dishes on the counter, all of which seemed to have different foods sitting steaming within them, some of which Otto was struggling to immediately recognise. As in the dining hall, the smell from all of these foods was delicious, but slightly over-powering, with the scents of hundreds of different herbs, spices and seasonings all competing for the nose's full attention. As the queue continued to move the first of the new group of students to be served was Franz, who, having put on an impressive burst of speed as they approached the dining hall, had managed somehow to be the first of them to join the queue.

The queue advanced steadily and Otto and Wing quickly chose from the assortment of foods on display, grabbed cutlery and moved away from the counter and through the exit to the dining hall. Looking around the cavern they noticed that Franz and the American girl were already seated at a table, and Otto and Wing headed over to join them. Franz was eating quickly and noisily, almost seeming to suck the food from the fork as it went into his mouth. The American girl, by contrast, was prodding at the food on her plate with an unhappy look on her face.

'Mind if we join you?' Otto asked. The American girl looked up from her plate.

'Help yourself,' she replied glumly, returning to her food-prodding with a sigh.

As Otto and Wing sat down a small, timid voice behind Otto asked, 'Can I sit here?' The bald boy with the thick glasses stood there, indicating the seat next to Otto's.

'Please do,' Otto replied. The boy smiled and sat down. 'My name's Otto and this is Wing.' Otto gestured to Wing, who was not eating, just sitting staring with deep suspicion at the bowl in front of him. 'And you are . . .?'

'Nigel . . . Nigel Darkdoom,' the bald boy replied in a small voice. Otto fought very hard to stop himself from laughing at this rather incongruous name for this un-assuming boy. Wing, however, stopped contemplating his food and looked carefully at Nigel the moment he heard his name.

'Would you be related to the late Diabolus Darkdoom, by any chance?' Wing asked.

'Yes, he was my dad,' Nigel replied, looking embarrassed and slightly sad.

Otto had never heard of Diabolus Darkdoom, but judging by Wing's reaction he clearly should have done.

'My own father was a great admirer of his work,' Wing continued. 'He told me many tales of Darkdoom's adventures; it is a great honour to meet his son.' Nigel began to look even more uncomfortable, his face turning bright red. 'It was a sad day when he fell in action. I am truly sorry for your loss,' Wing said sincerely.

'Thank you,' Nigel gave a weak smile, 'though I'll never be the man my dad was. He always used to say that I should just have more confidence in myself, but I don't think I'll ever really be a Darkdoom at heart.'

Wing nodded. 'I too know what it is like to live in your father's shadow.'

'Who's living in whose shadow?' Laura asked as she sat down in the last free seat at the table.

'I think we're all living in his,' Otto commented, nodding in the direction of Dr Nero.

'Aye, I think you're right there.' Laura sat down and gestured at her generous lunch. 'Well, at least H.I.V.E. seems to know that the way to a person's heart is through their stomach.'

'Or about two centimetres to the right of their sternum,' Otto replied, smiling at Laura. Wing chuckled and shook his head. The American girl put her fork down and sighed.

'What I don't get is how they've managed to keep this place a secret for so long. I mean there's hundreds of people here who we've seen already, and from what it said in that movie H.I.V.E. has been going for nearly forty years. Surely somebody would have spilled the beans about all this by now?' She picked up her fork again and carried on nudging the untouched food around her plate.

'There are ways to keep the big secrets for a very long time, my father is often saying,' Franz offered, tipping up his bowl to capture the last morsels of his lunch. 'Perhaps he was talking about the big secret that he was once a student here himself, or that he was going to send me to this terrible place.' He waved at the walls around him.

Laura looked puzzled. 'That's the thing that I can't understand. Why would my mum and dad agree to this? I'm not some kind of junior super-villain and I can't see them approving of all this, it's just too weird. I mean it's not like some bloke turned up on our front doorstep and said, sorry to bother you, Mr and Mrs Brand, but if you don't mind we'd like to abduct your daughter and train her to take over the world with all the other little megalomaniacs.'

'Well, somebody must've signed you up,' the American girl said. 'If my mom and dad sent me here then you can bet there's a good reason. They always said I'd go to the best school that they could find, so I guess this must be it. My dad was always telling me that nothing was too good for his Shelby.'

It struck Otto that Shelby's parents may just have been looking for a school that would keep her under lock and key for a few years in a secure location a very long way away from them. Still, there was something about Shelby that bothered Otto. He had always been unnaturally good at spotting a liar and something about her just didn't ring true. He suspected she was hiding something, as if the unpleasant persona she displayed was an act. He resolved to keep a slightly closer eye on her and see if he could get any closer to the truth.

There was one other question that had been bothering Otto. Who had picked him? Somebody had to have selected him for this, and even now was footing the bill for his new life at H.I.V.E. The problem was, he had no idea who or why. Just one more question to add to the rapidly lengthening list, he thought.

'My mum will have signed me up,' said Nigel. 'She's always wanted me to follow in my father's footsteps. She was always saying that one day I'd learn to be like him. I suppose this is what she was talking about.' He didn't seem particularly enthusiastic about the prospect of becoming Darkdoom Jr.

'Well, I suspect we've all done something to earn a place at H.I.V.E.,' said Otto. 'It's just a question of figuring out what it was.' He was almost certain that the events of the last few days explained his own presence on the island, but he was curious to know what special characteristic marked the others out as H.I.V.E. recruits.

Laura looked slightly uncomfortable with this topic of conversation and Otto suspected that, despite what she had said, she too probably had a pretty good idea about whatever it was that she'd done to deserve a place at H.I.V.E.

Wing was staying strangely silent throughout this, and Otto wondered what it was about him that had attracted H.I.V.E.'s attention. For the moment, at least, it wasn't something he appeared to want to share with the other students.

'What about you?' Franz pointed his fork at Otto. 'What have you done?'

Otto had feared that this might come up, but he wasn't sure he wanted to share that with the others right now. He didn't know them well enough to tell them everything just yet.

'I'm not sure. I suppose we'll find out eventually what we did to deserve this.' Time for a change of subject, Otto thought. 'Anyway, did you see that classroom on the way here with all the –'

Otto was interrupted by a firm tap on his shoulder. The others at the table were all staring wide-eyed at something behind him. Slowly he turned round in his seat. Standing there were two massive boys. They both had blond hair that was cropped close to their skulls and what they might have lacked in height they more than made up for in width. Neither of them appeared to have necks, their massive shoulders seeming to blend seamlessly into their jawline. They both wore blue overalls that were struggling to accommodate their bulky frames, which wasn't to say that they were fat; in fact they appeared to be made of solid muscle. Otto thought back to the briefing earlier that morning – blue overalls meant Henchman stream.

'Dis is our table,' the first brute said, 'move . . . now.' He stared down at Otto, his look seeming to suggest that doing what he asked was a good idea, unless you happened to be a fan of the sound of snapping bones. Your own bones specifically. Otto stared back at him.

'I'm sorry,' Otto replied, 'but I don't speak gorilla. You're going to need an interpreter.'

The hulking boy's face turned dark. 'Whadidchoo say?'

Otto sighed. 'I said that your limited communication skills are going to make it very difficult for us to have a meaningful inter-species conversation.' Otto heard the scraping sound of the others at the table sliding their chairs away from his.

The henchman student turned to his companion. 'I fink this little maggot is making fun of us, Mr Block.'

'I agree, Mr Tackle. Dat is a shame. We will have to show him what happens to maggots what don't do what we tell dem to,' the other boy replied.

With that the boy called Tackle turned Otto's chair around and picked it up *with Otto still sitting in it*. He didn't appear even to be straining himself as he brought the still-seated Otto up to his eye level, as if examining him more closely. Wing started to get up from his chair but Otto shot him a quick look, shaking his head slightly, and he sat back down, a look of concern on his face.

'He is a funny little man though. It would be a shame to break him.' Tackle gave Otto an evil grin.

Otto returned his smile. 'You couldn't hold me a little lower, could you? It's just that you're breathing right on me and I've just eaten.' Otto knew that it probably wasn't wise to wind Tackle up like this, but if there was one thing he hated it was a bully.

'I fink you might want to shut up now. It's gonna be hard for you to talk anyway with a mouthful of teeth.'

'Oh, do be quiet.' Otto reached out and jammed his index finger into the soft flesh beneath Tackle's ear.

There was a fleeting look of astonishment on Tackle's face and then his eyes rolled upwards and he collapsed, dropping the chair with a loud bang that echoed around the cavern and jarred Otto's spine. All over the room heads turned in their direction as the wide-eyed Block stared in amazement at his friend who was now gently snoring on the floor.

'You're dead,' Block shouted, and with a murderous look on his face he charged at Otto like an enraged rhino. Otto quickly stood up. He had a horrible feeling that he might have bitten off more than he could chew.

There was a blur of movement to Otto's right and suddenly Wing was standing between him and the charging henchman. Block had no chance to react as Wing dropped low and swept one foot out in an arc that took the thug's feet cleanly out from under him. Little more than a projectile now, the giant boy sailed through the air, his chin coming down on the edge of the table with a crack. The other students scattered as the table tipped, the remains of their half-eaten meals sliding down it and covering the snoozing Tackle and the groaning Block.

Otto was astonished by the speed with which Wing had moved.

'Are you all right, Otto?' he asked.

'I'm fine,' Otto replied, 'at least for the moment.' He

looked past Wing at the advancing figures of Dr Nero and the Contessa.

'Oh dear, oh dear, oh dear.' Nero looked down at the unconscious henchman and his dazed companion. 'It would seem that you have started to make friends already, Mr Malpense.'

Otto feared that Dr Nero knowing his name was probably not a good thing.

'They started it,' said Laura indignantly, pointing at Tackle and Block.

'And the two of you finished it, apparently.' Nero gave Otto and Wing a long stare and then prodded the unconscious Tackle with his toe. Block, groaning, rose to his feet, his head covered in gravy.

'Mr Block, take Mr Tackle to sick bay and have them check you both over,' Nero instructed.

Don't bother, Otto thought, head injuries shouldn't worry these two.

Block gave Otto and Wing a murderous look and then taking Tackle by both arms he began to drag his still gently snoring companion from the hall.

'What is the meaning of this, gentlemen?' the Contessa demanded. 'H.I.V.E. will not tolerate *unauthorised* violence between students, especially students that have only been here for a matter of hours.'

'I was just introducing myself,' Otto replied innocently.

'I'm afraid I appear to have inadvertently offended them somehow.'

'Forgive me, Mr Malpense,' Nero said, fixing Otto with a piercing look, 'if I find it hard to believe you would do anything by accident. This is hardly a promising start to your first day, is it?'

'No, Dr Nero. It won't happen again.' Otto looked down at the floor, doing his best impression of an apologetic child. While he might be prepared to pick a fight with two shaved apes like Block and Tackle he wasn't quite prepared to take on Dr Nero just yet. Better that the good Doctor believed that he was prepared to toe the line for now.

'See that it doesn't. I would hate to have to take disciplinary measures.' Nero paused. 'I don't like to see young lives wasted.' Otto didn't think that he was talking about missed educational opportunities.

Chapter 4

The rest of the afternoon seemed to pass in a blur. They were hurried from one area of H.I.V.E. to the next, being shown where all of the school's key facilities were and the locations of the classrooms that would play host to their first few lessons. Notably, they'd been taken to the sick bay, which seemed to Otto more like a fully equipped miniature hospital than some dusty room used by a school nurse. There had been a nasty moment when they'd arrived at the sick bay just as Block and Tackle were leaving following their check-up. They'd given Otto and Wing looks as they walked past the group which, for the first time, almost made them grateful that the Contessa was there. It left them in little doubt that they would be very wise to avoid an unscheduled meeting with them in some distant deserted corridor of the school.

They'd also been taken to the physical training cavern, where they'd seen groups of exhausted students being put through their paces by gym teachers who looked more like drill instructors. As soon as one group completed the full assault course that ran the length of the cavern they were scaling long ropes that hung from the ceiling. Otto had never been a particular fan of intense physical exercise, so he was not really looking forward to his first session in this cavern. Wing, however, seemed to be delighted with the array of exercise machines and training equipment, even strangely remarking at one point that they reminded him of home.

Throughout this the Contessa had continued to explain the workings of H.I.V.E. to them and answered most of their many questions about the school. Otto had been more interested in the questions that she avoided answering than the ones that she had rattled off an obviously well-practised response to. As before, she had remained oddly reluctant to answer anything relating to transport off the island or communications with families, but he had been interested to note that she also wouldn't discuss exactly how many people were on the island or what source of power they used. He had considered pressing her for answers to these queries, but had thought better of it when Wing reminded him that the only answer he was likely to get from the Contessa would almost certainly cause temporary confusion and amnesia.

And so, eventually, they had ended up back at Plotting Room Two, where the tour had started that morning, all, once again, seated around the large black table. Only one thing had changed about the room since that morning. Arranged neatly on the table in front of each of the students were what looked like small, matt-black PDAs with the H.I.V.E. logo in silver on the front. The Contessa stood at the end of the table and addressed them.

'So, children, that completes your introductory tour of H.I.V.E. I've no doubt that some of you will have found it difficult to take in all that you have seen today, but as you spend more time here you will find that you quickly become used to life at H.I.V.E. I'm sure you also have many unanswered questions, and with that in mind the last thing I'd like to introduce you to before you are taken to your new quarters is this.' She held up a device identical to the ones that sat on the table in front of each of the children. 'This is your H.I.V.E. personal digital assistant, more commonly known to the students and staff as a Blackbox. This device is designed to provide all of the assistance you need in getting used to life at H.I.V.E. and should prove invaluable to you over the months to come. Take good care of it and, whatever you do, do NOT lose it. Please pick up your Blackboxes and open them, like so.' The Contessa flipped open the cover on the front of the device.

They all dutifully did as instructed and there was a chorus of bleeps from around the room as the tiny machines started up. The screen on Otto's machine displayed the H.I.V.E. logo for a couple of seconds, which then vanished to be replaced by the familiar blue wireframe face of H.I.V.E.mind.

'Good afternoon, Mr Malpense. How may I be of assistance?' the machine's soft voice enquired.

All around the room H.I.V.E.mind could be heard greeting each of the group by name.

'Your Blackbox provides a direct mobile interface with H.I.V.E.mind and you may consult him at any time of the day or night for help or advice. He can provide you with all of the details of your timetable and any outstanding schoolwork that you may be due to complete, as well as advising you on any other aspect of school life that you may be unsure about.' The Contessa continued, 'The Blackbox is essentially indestructible: it is waterproof, shock-proof, fire-proof, radiation-proof and will, I am told, even function in a vacuum. This is your single most important piece of school equipment and must be carried with you at all times. Failure to do so is a serious breach of school rules and offenders will be punished accordingly.'

Otto was willing to bet that this strict rule meant that it would be a lot easier to track the movements of a student who had to carry their Blackbox with them at all times. He also found the name of the device worrying, given that Blackboxes were normally used to determine what went wrong in an air disaster only after everyone aboard an aircraft was dead. He wondered if the children's Blackboxes would serve a similar purpose if something 'unfortunate' should happen to them. Still, it was a direct link to H.I.V.E.mind and that could certainly prove useful.

'Now, as promised, I shall escort you to your accommodation block and you can get settled into your quarters. Please follow me.' The Contessa headed towards the Plotting Room door as the group stood up to follow her.

☻☻☻

'This,' the Contessa said, 'is accommodation area seven.'

The large high-roofed cavern had an impressive open stone-floored atrium in the centre, with a waterfall at one end, tumbling from a small cave near the roof and down the wall into a crystal-clear pool. Arranged around the atrium were groups of comfortable sofas and armchairs, many of which were occupied by students who appeared to come from a cross-section of all streams, judging by their uniforms. Some were sat alone working, flicking through books or scribbling in note pads, while others sat around in groups, engrossed in conversation or playing games. There were even some swimming in the pool at the base of the waterfall.

Around the walls of the cavern were wide balconies on four different levels. Strange twisting vines and other tropical plants hung from each balcony, and elevators in glass tubes could be seen ferrying people quickly between the different floors. Opening on to each balcony were rows of identical white doors, which would occasionally hiss open and shut as students came and went.

'This is where you will spend much of your time when not in classes. There are many communal facilities in this area that you may wish to take advantage of, including libraries and games rooms, but I shall leave it to your new block monitor to explain this all to you in more detail. Now, where is Mr Khan?' The Contessa looked around the room. 'Ah, there he is. Come along.' The Contessa set off across the atrium.

'Well, this seems . . . erm . . . nice,' Nigel said as they made their way across the broad atrium in pursuit of the Contessa.

'As long as we all don't have to share one bathroom,' Shelby replied.

Otto noted that this area seemed to be designed on the same grand scale as all of the other facilities within H.I.V.E. that they had seen so far. It was as if the architect of the facility had been given a brief to make sure that the students were overwhelmed by its size. No doubt this was done deliberately to give the students the impression of being very small individual parts in a much larger machine. It was hard not to be impressed by such grandiose construction, but Otto reminded himself that big did not necessarily mean better.

The Contessa halted beside a group of three sofas arranged around a low table. Sitting in these seats were three older students, two boys and a girl, who were engaged in such a heated discussion that they did not notice the Contessa's approach.

'I don't care what you say. He's just a man, he's not indestructible,' said a tall black girl wearing a white uniform.

'Then how come he's still around after all these years, survived all those attempts to eliminate him?' asked a thin boy with a crooked nose and a vertical scar across one eye. His black jumpsuit marked him out as an Alpha.

'More to the point, why doesn't he seem to have aged at all since he first appeared? He should be sixty or seventy years old now, but he still looks like he's in his thirties,' offered the third student, a handsome Indian boy with long dark hair that fell to his shoulders and a goatee beard, trimmed into an immaculate triangle, on his chin. He too wore the black jumpsuit of an Alpha stream student.

'Maybe he's not actually the same guy as when he first appeared. Maybe they just alter a younger man's appearance to match his every few years and quietly replace him,' the black girl replied.

'Oh, come on, Jo, that's ridiculous,' the Indian boy shot back. 'As if people wouldn't be able to see the difference. Look, I'm telling you, he's still the same guy, and if –'

'Ahem.' The Contessa cleared her throat and the boy turned, startled. Seeing her standing there, he immediately leapt to his feet.

'Oh, sorry, Contessa. We didn't see you there, we were just discussing . . . er . . .' The boy looked at his companions, as if willing them to complete his sentence for him.

'I know perfectly well what you were discussing, Mr Khan, and I hardly think that it's a suitable topic when there are new recruits present, do you?' She gave him a stern look.

'No, Contessa, you're right.' The boy looked slightly embarrassed to be reprimanded like this in front of the other students.

'Good, now let me introduce you to our latest Alpha recruits.' She indicated the group standing behind her. 'They're all going to be residents in area seven, and I thought you could explain the set-up of their accommodation to them.'

'Of course, Contessa.' The boy turned his attention to the new students, giving them a broad smile.

Otto noticed that there were six studs on the boy's collar arranged in the same pattern as normally seen on dice. The other two students who had been arguing with the boy also had six studs on their collar and Otto guessed that, like the single stud on his collar, they indicated a student's current school year. The only difference was that the studs on Khan's uniform were silver, which Otto assumed reflected his position of relative authority.

'Very well.' The Contessa turned back to the group. 'I shall leave you all in Mr Khan's capable hands. I'm sure I will see you all again soon in class. Do be sure to check your Blackboxes for details of your timetable. Lessons start first thing tomorrow morning. DON'T be late.'

Otto couldn't help but feel slightly relieved as the Contessa walked away.

'So you're the new magg— er . . . first years, are you? Well, welcome to H.I.V.E. My name's Tahir Khan and I'm the monitor for this accommodation area.' Tahir seemed friendly, but Otto was starting to realise how deceptive appearances could be in this place.

'If your first day's been anything like mine was I'm sure you have about a thousand questions that urgently need answering, but I'm afraid that I probably can't tell you much more than you already know right now. Best thing to do is to use your Blackbox to ask H.I.V.E.mind anything you're not sure about. Don't worry if it all seems a bit much at the moment, you learn quickly around here. You have to.' He grinned at the group. 'So why don't I show you one of the rooms and then you can all get settled in before dinner. Come on.'

He set off across the cavern towards one of the elevators. It was a bit of a squeeze getting them all in but eventually the doors closed and they shot up to the fourth floor. Here Tahir stopped in front of one of the white doors.

'This is a Standard Twin Habitation Unit, but we call them cells,' he said with a wry grin. 'But don't worry, that's just a nickname. They're quite comfortable really.' Tahir placed his hand on the smooth panel set into the wall next to the door, which briefly illuminated and bleeped. The door slid open.

'Now we won't all fit in here, so just gather round the doorway and I'll show you the basics,' Tahir continued, stepping into the room.

The room itself was outfitted in white and silver and looked comfortable, if a little cramped. Nearest the door were two white desks, one on either side of the room, with a monitor, mouse and keyboard on each. Sitting alongside the computers on both these desks were identical piles of books and a pile of pens, notebooks and other stationery. Then came twin stainless steel closets, again mirroring each other, recessed into each wall and, finally, two single beds. Between the beds, set into the rear wall, was another white door.

'This place is probably the nearest thing you'll get to any privacy round here, so make the most of it. The computers you can see on the desks are directly interfaced with Big Blue – sorry,' Tahir apologised, noting the momentary looks of confusion on some of their faces, 'that's what some of us call H.I.V.E.mind. Then you've got your closets. Hang your uniform in your wardrobe each night and you'll find a clean one there in the morning. And before you ask, no, I don't know how they get in to change them without anyone ever noticing. They just seem to materialise.'

Interesting, Otto thought.

'Then you've got your beds and through the other door your bathroom. I'm not going to explain how everything works in there. You're all Alphas, not grunts, so I shouldn't have to.' Otto detected more than a hint of smugness, arrogance, even, in the way that Tahir said this. He seemed just a little too proud to be wearing the black uniform.

'All the rooms are the same so most of us make some attempt to liven them up a bit. Just one piece of advice, don't paint anything. The janitor tends to get upset about that and you don't want to upset him, believe me.' He stepped back out of the room and the door slid shut behind him automatically. 'All the doors are keyed to these palm readers.' He indicated the panel he had placed his hand on a few moments before. 'So there's no need for keys, which is good because it's unlikely you're going to lose your right hand. At least not in your first year, anyway . . .' Worryingly, Tahir didn't appear to be joking.

'Use your Blackboxes to find out from H.I.V.E.mind which room is yours and who your room-mate will be. You've got about an hour before dinner so take this time to have a look around. If you need any help, you can usually find me somewhere around the atrium or you can just give me a call on your box. OK, that's about it for now. I've got to get moving or I'll miss Grappletag practice. Good luck.' He winked at the assembled group and strode away down the balcony.

Several of those around Otto pulled out their Blackboxes and queried H.I.V.E.mind about which room they had been assigned. Otto followed suit, flipping the device open.

'Good afternoon, Mr Malpense. How may I be of assistance?' the blue face enquired.

'Good afternoon to you too, H.I.V.E.mind. I need to know which room I have been assigned, please,' Otto replied.

'You are assigned to accommodation area seven, room 4.7. Will there be anything else?' H.I.V.E.mind asked.

'No, that's all for now. Thanks, H.I.V.E.mind.' The blue face disappeared.

Otto noticed that Wing was also checking his Blackbox and as he talked to the machine a broad grin spread across his face. He noticed Otto looking at him.

'It appears we are to be room-mates, Otto,' he said, still smiling.

'I hope you don't snore,' Otto laughed.

'Like a chainsaw, my friend, like a chainsaw,' Wing replied, grinning.

☢☢☢

Room 4.7 was exactly the same as the room they had been shown, just as Tahir had said it would be. Otto sat at his desk, idly flicking through one of the neatly stacked textbooks. Studying their titles, Otto doubted that they were set texts at any other school in the world. *Death-traps: Their Use and Care, Effective Threats, Elementary Evil, Global Domination: What You Need to Know!, A Beginner's Guide to Doomsday Weapons* and several others that he'd not yet had a chance to look at.

Wing sat on his bed studying his Blackbox intently.

'Well, what have we got tomorrow, then?' Otto asked.

'The first lesson is Villainy Studies with . . .' Wing

checked the machine again, 'Dr Nero. Well that should at least be an *interesting* start to the day.'

Otto raised an eyebrow at his new room-mate.

'Then what?'

Wing checked the Blackbox again. 'Then we have Tactical Education with Colonel Francisco. That's followed by Practical Technology with Professor Pike first thing after lunch and then Stealth and Evasion with Ms Leon.'

'Sounds like a highly educational first day. I can hardly wait to get started.' Otto grinned, placing the textbook he'd been leafing through back on the desk. He moved over and sat on his own bed facing Wing. Beckoning him to lean closer, he said softly, 'We have to get out of here, off this island, as soon as possible.'

Wing frowned slightly. 'Agreed. H.I.V.E. is certainly impressive, but I have no desire to spend the next few years of my life as a virtual prisoner.'

'My sentiments exactly,' replied Otto, nodding. 'The problem is how. I've not seen any sign of an exit to the surface and I've been looking for one all day.'

'As have I, but even if we were to find an exit, what would we do once we got to the surface? I doubt that we would be given enough time to construct a raft.'

'We might not need to. Did you notice the sign pointing to the submarine pen earlier?' Otto asked, his voice dropping to a whisper. He'd searched the room thoroughly as soon as the door had closed but he still wasn't sure if the room was bugged or not. It looked clean, but until he knew for certain, he had decided that he would work on the assumption that any unguarded conversations should not be treated as private.

Wing looked at Otto carefully and replied in a whisper, 'Yes, I saw it, but are you seriously proposing that we use a stolen submarine as our escape vehicle? How would we pilot it? Somehow I suspect that requests for submariner lessons will arouse a certain amount of suspicion.'

'I could do it, I don't need lessons,' Otto said calmly.

'You know how to pilot a submarine?' Wing arched one eyebrow.

'No, but I'm a quick learner,' Otto replied with a slight smile.

'You would have to be. You'll forgive me if I choose not to stake my life on your ability to improvise.' Wing seemed almost irritated that Otto was suggesting something so ridiculous.

Otto suspected that Wing probably thought he was losing his mind. He could understand his disbelief, but Otto knew that if he could get a couple of uninterrupted minutes to examine any vehicle he'd be able to pilot it. Assuming that it was physically possible for one person to do it of course, but they would cross that bridge when they came to it. The problem would be convincing Wing that he could do it. 'Trust me, I know what I'm doing' wasn't going to cut it when he was effectively asking his new friend to put his life in his hands.

'Anyway, it doesn't really matter until we get some idea of what the security around the submarine pen is like,' Otto said. 'The fact that it's so openly signposted means that our hosts are confident that it's secure.'

Wing nodded. 'Indeed, security is clearly taken quite seriously around here.'

That was something of an understatement. There had seemingly been security cameras in the corner of every room during the tour. Steel spheres, the size of a tennis ball with a single black eye surrounded by blue LEDs, intended presumably to remind students that these were the eyes of the all-seeing H.I.V.E.mind. A person would have to be invisible to make their way around H.I.V.E. undetected, or may be . . . Otto felt a familiar tingling as the seed of a plan began to germinate in his head.

'Well, let's just keep our eyes and ears open for now and see if any other opportunities present themselves. Anyway,' continued Otto, 'I haven't thanked you properly for saving my skin at lunch today. I'm not sure what I'd have done without your help.'

'You seemed to be handling the situation quite admirably,' Wing replied. 'You certainly subdued your first assailant efficiently.'

'You just have to know which buttons to press,' Otto smiled. 'Or, more accurately, what vulnerable clusters of sensitive nerve-endings to press.'

'I fear we may have drawn unwelcome attention with our actions. Dr Nero did not seem pleased,' said Wing, frowning slightly.

Otto knew what Wing meant. Otto rarely met people who he truly considered to be his equal, so when he did it meant that they were people to be added to the pile marked 'Dangerous'. At the moment Dr Nero was right at the top of that pile. Otto would have to discreetly find out as much as he possibly could about Nero without attracting his closer attention. He felt certain that you didn't want to be top of the Doctor's 'Things to Do' list. Unbidden a mental image formed in Otto's head of a giant Dr Nero using a magnifying glass to focus the burning rays of the sun on to a little white-haired ant. He dismissed the disturbing image from his mind and rose from the bed. 'Well, here's hoping that we don't have a repeat performance at dinner. Speaking of which, we'd better get going or we'll be late.'

☻☻☻

Wing hadn't been joking about the snoring. Otto lay in his bed with a hastily fashioned toilet-paper plug in each ear. He could no longer hear Wing, but he swore he could feel his bed vibrating slightly.

Dinner had thankfully passed uneventfully. Block and Tackle had been there but they'd been seated at a distant table with a group of similarly hulking brutes, all of them wearing the same blue henchman overalls. Save for a couple of murderous stares when either Wing or Otto had inadvertently caught their eye they had steered well clear of the new recruits. The security guards patrolling the cavern probably had something to do with that. It also became clear that the staff did not eat dinner with the students since the top table had remained empty throughout the course of the meal. Otto wondered what their evening dining arrangements might be.

After dinner he and Wing had spent a couple of hours exploring the accommodation block's facilities. This had included an abortive game of darts which was abandoned after Wing hit nine bull's-eyes in a row. The more time Otto spent with Wing the more the large, well-spoken Asian boy surprised him. He had tried gently probing Wing for more details of his background but when Wing had seemed reluctant to discuss the topic Otto had dropped it, not wanting his curiosity to damage the friendship that was developing between them. After all, if they didn't come up with a plan and do something about their current situation they'd have six long years to find out all about each other.

The plan that Otto was nurturing was still slowly forming in his mind, but the more he concentrated on it the more elusive the details seemed. He knew that he had to just stop consciously thinking about it and over time the problems with the scheme would resolve themselves, but he was impatient – he felt trapped.

As he lay in bed, blissfully deaf to the ungodly noise coming from Wing's side of the room, he found himself mentally going over the events of the weeks leading up to his arrival at H.I.V.E. Looking back on it now, he supposed it had all started with the letter . . .

Chapter 5

'They can't do this!' Otto shouted, waving at the letter that lay on the desk in front of him. 'I've spent years getting this place running just right, and now this!'

He stood up from the battered leather office chair behind his desk and paced around the room. The old attic where he stood was lined with shelves full of books and the scattered remains of hundreds of different electronic devices. Standing in the centre of the room was a middle-aged woman in an expensive suit. Her red eyes betrayed the fact she had been crying recently.

'Oh, I just don't know what to do, Mr Malpense. I brought you the letter as soon as I read it. These horrible people are going to close the orphanage down and there's nothing we can do. I've spent my whole life working here and I just don't know what will become of me if they close it down . . . oh, Mr Malpense, this is terrible.' With great heaving sobs, she burst into tears again.

Otto put his hand on her shoulder. 'Don't worry, Mrs McReedy, I'll think of something. They needn't think that they're shutting us down without a fight. St Sebastian's isn't finished yet.' He handed Mrs McReedy a hankie from his pocket and she proceeded to blow her nose explosively.

'I'm sorry, Mr Malpense, but you know how worried I get about these things.' She sniffed and dabbed at the corners of her eyes with the hankie. 'And it's not that I don't have faith in you, but that letter seems so final. I just don't see what we can do.'

Otto picked up the letter from the desk again and, scanned its contents. There was a lot of overblown language and official-sounding jargon, but it all boiled down to just one thing. St Sebastian's orphanage was to be closed down in two weeks' time and that was the local council's final decision. There was mention of missed performance targets and restructuring of local childcare provision but these just sounded like excuses to Otto. They were going to close HIS orphanage, and he had just a fortnight to persuade them otherwise.

☻☻☻

He had arrived at St Sebastian's twelve years before, left in a cradle on the doorstep in the middle of the night with no form of identification except a single piece of

84

white card with the handwritten name Otto Malpense on it. The staff of the orphanage were used to dealing with these kinds of situations and had gone through the usual motions of reporting the nocturnal delivery to the police in the hope that they might be able to track down Otto's parents. The search, however, had proved fruitless; there was not a trace to be found of whoever had abandoned Otto on that dark, stormy night. So, there being no other place for him, the strange little white-haired baby had been taken in and St Sebastian's had become his new home.

When Otto first arrived there, St Sebastian's was a long way from being the most well-staffed or -equipped orphanage in London. It had been built over one hundred and fifty years previously and the tired old house showed many scars from its long years of busy occupation. Its ornate façade was covered in ivy and the roof had clearly been patched many times over with whatever materials were immediately to hand. The interior of the building had just as many problems. The water pipes clanked and rumbled, the floors were uneven and creaky and it was too big and old to really keep it thoroughly clean so dust seemed to gather everywhere. The children's dormitories were old-fashioned; each lined with steel-framed bunk beds and served by only one cramped, rusty bathroom for every twenty or thirty children. Many of the older sections of the building had proved to be too expensive to renovate over the years and so there were what seemed like miles of abandoned, dusty corridors that were rarely, if ever, used by anyone. Somehow St Sebastian's had managed to avoid closure over the years, possibly because it was one of the only orphanages left in the area. Nevertheless, the money available to the orphanage had dwindled as the years went by and this had led to the accelerated decline of the grand old building. Indeed, the staff seemed to spend as much time carrying out makeshift repairs as they did looking after the children.

At first Otto had seemed to be quite a normal child, with the obvious exception of his unusually coloured hair, but as he got slightly older people had started to notice that there was something a little bit odd about him. At the age of three he taught himself to read. He sat on the floor of the common room staring for hours at several of the books that older children had left lying around, his face frozen in a look of intense concentration. The staff had thought this was highly amusing.

'Look at him! He looks just like he's reading,' one of the staff would say.

'Oh, he's just copying what the other children do,' another would reply.

But he wasn't just imitating what he had seen other

people do. As he sat staring at the letters on the page it was almost as if his brain just *understood* them. At first the words had meant nothing to him, but as he stared at the pages their meaning became clearer and clearer to him, as if the knowledge was somehow just growing in his head. Not only that but he could remember every last word of every page that he had looked at. It was as though his brain was sucking the knowledge, vampire-like, from the books.

Then there was the time, when he was five, that he had taken Mrs McReedy's phone apart. It was not unusual for the children at St Sebastian's to dismantle things like this, but Otto didn't just take it apart. As he sat surrounded by the scattered components of the phone he could see exactly what each piece was supposed to do and how, when they were fitted back together correctly, their function could be improved. In fact when he did finally put the phone back together again it worked better than it ever had before. It wasn't until two months later when the next phone bill arrived that Mrs McReedy realised that none of the calls she had made for the past eight weeks had cost her anything. She had queried this with the phone company who informed her that their systems didn't make mistakes of that kind and she should stop wasting their time claiming that she had made calls when she clearly hadn't.

When he was very young, before he started school, Otto spent many hours slowly exploring every nook and cranny of the mysterious old building. He had an uncanny knack for sneaking away unnoticed. He would sit down with the other pre-school children in the common room and appear to join in with their games. Then someone would call the member of staff away for a moment or their attention would wander for a few seconds and before they knew it Otto would have vanished. The first time that this happened it had triggered a full-scale panic as the staff of the orphanage turned the building upside down searching for him. Not a trace could be found anywhere of the little boy, despite a thorough search of the building and grounds. Mrs McReedy had been just about to call the police and officially report him missing when he had toddled back into the common room. He had been missing for several hours and was covered from head to toe in dust and grime. When asked where he had been all day he had given Mrs McReedy a puzzled look and replied, 'Here.' Further questioning had proven useless. Eventually, this became such a common occurrence with Otto that the staff gave up looking for him, knowing that he would eventually reappear, none the worse for his travels and surprised, irritated even, by their concern.

The staff of the orphanage weren't the only people

who witnessed Otto's slightly odd behaviour. Just down the street from the orphanage was the library, one of the oldest and largest in London. Like St Sebastian's, it was a grand old Gothic building that dated back hundreds of years and for Otto it soon felt like a second home. Mrs McReedy had given up trying to find new books in the orphanage for this strange little boy who read so quickly that it looked as if he was just checking the page numbers. So she would take him down to the library whenever she could where he would be placed in the charge of Mr Littleton, the librarian, a good friend of Mrs McReedy. Mr Littleton was happy to keep an eye on Otto for her – the little boy was no trouble at all, he told her. He just sat flicking through the books all day, without a care in the world. Nobody, at least at first, believed that a child of Otto's age could actually be reading and understanding the books at that speed.

But he was, though it wasn't reading as most people understood it. In just the same way as when he learnt to read in the first place it was as if the knowledge contained within each book he read was leaping straight from the page into his brain. He couldn't explain it, but the more he read the more he knew and the more he knew the better his understanding of what he had already read. And he read literally everything, from Tolkien to Tolstoy, from Sun Tzu to the *Sunday Times*, often choosing a specific section of the library each day and devouring whole bookcases without pausing. The staff at the library would joke with each other about the odd little boy who just sat on the floor, surrounded by piles of books and papers, pretending to read. Perhaps he's not quite right in the head, they would say to each other, but at least he's safe and happy here. All except Mr Littleton, who, over time, grew to realise that Otto *was* reading the books, absorbing them, almost. He tried to tell this to his colleagues but they just started to think that he was as odd as this strange little boy. Occasionally, when Mr Littleton happened upon Otto sitting in the aisles, he would stop, pluck a particular book from the shelves and hand it to him.

'Don't miss this one; you've got to read this.'

'Thank you, Mr Littleton,' Otto would reply each time, smiling at the elderly librarian with that peculiarly adult expression of his and adding the book to the top of one of the piles surrounding him.

All of which made traditional schooling rather irrelevant for Otto. The other orphans were normally sent for lessons at the local school but it quickly became clear that Otto was a little more *advanced* than his peers. His reading in the library had covered so many different subjects that by the time he was ten years old he had a better understanding of their subjects than most of his teachers. His teachers, for their part, had not taken kindly to being repeatedly corrected by a ten-year-old boy and eventually, inevitably, the headmaster of the school had formally complained to Mrs McReedy. So she in turn had summoned Otto to her office.

'What am I going to do with you, Otto?' she said, looking concerned.

'Why, what's the matter, Mrs McReedy?' Otto replied, appearing genuinely uncertain what it was that he was supposed to have done.

She looked down at some papers on her desk. 'It appears that some of your teachers . . . well, *all* of your teachers, actually, have been complaining that you're disrupting classes. Is this true?' She looked sternly at him.

'Well, if you call exposing their woeful incompetence disruptive, then yes, I suppose I have.' Otto stared back at her. Over the past few years Mrs McReedy had become increasingly used to Otto talking like this – clever but rude – and she could see how it would drive his teachers mad.

'Otto, you are ten years old, you aren't qualified to say whether or not your teachers are doing a good job. None of the other children have the problems that you do,' she continued, looking slightly exasperated with him.

'I'm not like the other children, you know that. They just take so long to understand everything that I get bored waiting. It's not my fault if I'm better than them,' Otto replied matter of factly. 'I've already learnt everything that's being covered in classes and I'm starting to wonder if I should even be there.' He folded his arms defiantly.

'Don't be silly. Your education isn't something you can just ignore, Otto. What are you going to do when you leave here if you don't have any qualifications?' Mrs McReedy couldn't quite believe she was having this conversation with someone Otto's age.

'Oh, I'm sure I'll think of something, Mrs McReedy.' Otto knew that he didn't need to worry about qualifications and exams. They were for normal children and he was already quite aware that he was far from normal.

'So what do you suggest we do, then?' she asked, secretly hoping that he would actually have a useful suggestion since she was struggling to come up with an answer herself. If Otto's misbehaviour continued, he would be excluded from school and that would mean questions might be asked about her own care of the children.

'You could be my teacher,' Otto replied.

She gave him a condescending smile. 'It's a long time since I taught anyone, Otto, and if your teachers at school aren't good enough for you what good would I be?'

'Oh, I'm not suggesting that you actually try to teach me. I agree, that would be pointless. No, better just to say that you're going to give me private tuition here at the orphanage, in order to keep up appearances,' Otto said thoughtfully.

'Who would teach you then?' Mrs McReedy seemed slightly confused.

'I would,' he replied calmly. 'Most of the teachers at the school are just reading the textbooks out loud. I can do that myself, and a whole lot faster than they can. You would just say that you're giving me private lessons here. Nobody ever needs to know otherwise.' He looked pleased with the idea.

Mrs McReedy considered Otto's suggestion for a moment. It did make a certain kind of sense, even if it wasn't strictly honest. It was clear to anyone that met Otto that he didn't want or need a traditional education, and at least this way there wouldn't be any awkward questions asked about her orphanage. In fact, being seen as the teacher of an apparent child genius would do her reputation no harm at all. She eyed Otto carefully.

'Let's just say for a moment that we went with your plan. You'd have to tell everyone that I was giving you lessons, and only you and I would know the truth.'

'It would be our little secret, Mrs McReedy,' Otto smiled. 'I imagine there's some sort of grant paid to people who provide a first-class education to a boy like that. Quite a substantial grant, several thousand pounds a year I should think, at least . . .'

A switch seemed to flick in Mrs McReedy's brain. There was a brief look of calculation on her face and she struggled in vain to suppress a smile.

It wasn't just books or machines that Otto could understand at a glance, it was people too. When he talked to someone he could understand precisely what made them tick and what to say to get exactly what he wanted. In Mrs McReedy's case it was surprisingly easy – pride and greed – the two best instincts to appeal to when trying to manipulate anyone. Machiavelli had taught him that one.

'Oh, I'm sure it wouldn't be much.' Her face betrayed the fact that she appeared to know otherwise. 'Let me make some enquiries. I can't promise anything but it might be worth looking into the possibility, at least.'

'I do hope it's possible,' Otto replied. 'I just think it would be so much better for everyone.'

Me most of all, he thought to himself.

☻☻☻

It came as no surprise to Otto that the new arrangements for his education by Mrs McReedy were subsequently made with almost indecent haste. He also noticed that her clothes suddenly seemed more expensive, and he occasionally caught a glimpse of some new piece of jewellery glittering on her wrist or at her throat. Clearly he was a profitable student. He didn't mind her spending the money on herself – indeed, if it meant that she was as eager as he was to keep the details of their 'arrangement' to herself then so much the better.

And so it was that for the next three years Otto was free to do essentially as he pleased. He had meant what he had said when he spoke to Mrs McReedy – he really did plan to educate himself, and over the following months he set about that task with a vengeance. He continued to read everything he could get his hands on and started to experiment with building more and more complex devices and machines of his own design, testing the limits of his knowledge. Every time he encountered a problem he didn't understand he would find the answer or study the theory that might lead to an answer. As his experiments grew more complicated he soon found that he needed a larger private space where he could work in seclusion, and had set about converting the orphanage's cavernous attic space to that end. The narrow flight of stairs that led up to the roof space was tucked away in one corner of the top floor of the building and he was fairly sure, judging by the state of the room, that no one had been up there for years. It suited his purposes perfectly and he spent several weeks clearing out the junk that had accumulated in this abandoned space over the years, preparing the attic for his use. He had even decorated the room after a fashion.

He wasn't sure what had made him put the desk and large leather chair at one end of the room but, like the map of the world that hung on the wall above them, they just seemed right somehow.

In tandem with his ongoing studies he had also started to build up stronger relationships with the other children at St Sebastian's. At least the ones that he considered to be most useful. Many of the others, even those a few years older than Otto, seemed to regard him as some sort of leader for reasons that Otto didn't quite understand at first. The children, for their part, reasoned that here was a boy who apparently didn't have to go to school, who seemed in fact to be able to do exactly as he pleased whenever he wanted and whom Mrs McReedy seemed strangely reluctant to criticise. His example seemed to them to be an excellent one to follow.

St Sebastian's, however, had continued to fall into disrepair. There were even some sections of the building that had now crossed the line from being a bit battered and rickety to actually becoming genuinely unsafe. Otto was determined that he would try to arrest this process and had set about a new project of restoring as much of the old building as possible to its former glory. It wasn't that he rolled up his sleeves and got on with the repairs himself, which seemed to him to be dangerously close to hard work. Instead he employed the services of companies from all over London which seemed all too eager to believe that the BBC were making a programme about the renovation of the building and understandably provided their services free of charge to such a worthy cause. This new show, *Please, Think of the Children*, was, of course, a complete fabrication on Otto's part, but he had discovered that one could work wonders with a big lie, some headed notepaper and an anonymous PO Box address. The donations from companies did not stop at repair work, though. Over the next few months the orphanage received free books, DVDs, games consoles, TVs, stereos, sports equipment and a host of other well-meaning donations. Otto was not interested in keeping any of these things for himself – he knew that if he could keep the other children at St Sebastian's happy then he wouldn't have to worry about them sticking their noses too far into his business or drawing inspectors to the orphanage with tales of inadequate facilities or poor treatment.

Now, as he sat alone at his desk rereading the ominous letter that had arrived that morning, he began to suspect that all of his efforts might have been for nothing. He had only just managed, after years of work, to get St Sebastian's into a state that he was happy with, and now some faceless bureaucrat was trying to take all of this away from him. It would take for ever to recreate such an elegant set-up at a different orphanage and he had neither the time nor the inclination to start over from scratch like that. Indeed, without someone who was as easy to influence as Mrs McReedy running the orphanage it might not be possible at all. There must be a way to stop this, he just had to figure out what it was . . .

☙❦❧

'PM'S CHILDCARE CRUSADE' was the headline of the newspaper article that Otto sat reading. The article neatly summarised how the plans for wholesale changes to the nation's orphanages were part of a personal project for the Prime Minister and that he alone was the driving force behind the rapid journey of these new plans through parliament. The plans were not that popular with the rest of his party but the Prime Minister's personal backing had ensured that they were being pushed through regardless. Otto put the paper back down on his desk and considered the plan that was forming in his head. It was risky, audacious, stupid, even, but it was the only solution of the many he had considered that might work.

He pressed a button on a small intercom unit on his desk. There was a slight delay and then the voice of Mrs McReedy replied.

'Hello Otto. Is there something you need?' She still sounded upset.

'Yes, Mrs McReedy. Could you send Tom and Penny up, please?' Otto asked politely.

'Certainly, Otto.' The intercom went dead and Otto sat back in his chair, still analysing the finer details of his plan.

A few minutes later there was a soft knock at the attic door.

'Come in,' Otto said loudly, and Tom and Penny walked into the room. Tom was the older of the two; he was good-looking and tall for a boy of his age. Penny, meanwhile, was about the same age as Otto and looked like the sweetest, most innocent little girl that you could ever hope to meet. Anyone who met the pair of them would think that butter would not melt in their mouths. It would only be later that they would notice that the rest of the butter had mysteriously disappeared along with the silverware . . . and the DVD player.

'Morning, you two,' Otto addressed them both cheerfully. 'I've got a bit of a shopping list and I was wondering, if you weren't too busy, if you could just run out and pick up a few things for me.'

'Sure, Otto. What do you need?' Tom replied, apparently eager to help.

'Oh, nothing especially difficult, a few new components, a couple of books, some software, the usual kind of thing.' Otto offered a piece of paper to Penny. 'Everything's listed there; if there's anything you're not sure about just let me know.'

Penny read the list carefully. 'Shouldn't be a problem, Otto, might take a couple of days, though.'

Otto had chosen these two for this task carefully; they had certain unique skills that marked them out from the other children. Simply put, they seemed to be able to get their hands on just about anything that Otto needed, no matter how rare or obscure. He was reasonably confident that if he told them that he wanted the London Eye dismantled and rebuilt in the orphanage garden that they would at least give it a try. They both insisted that they never stole anything, though, and that their talent apparently lay in convincing other people to *give* them the things that they needed.

Otto always kept a sharp eye out for the children at the orphanage who, like these two, had unique 'talents'. In his experience people were far more willing to trust children, a belief that when properly exploited could prove extremely useful. Add in the fact that they were orphans and they'd soon have most sympathetic adults eating out of the palm of their hands. Otto discouraged the children from taking part in any overt criminal activity, as it was far too likely to attract the wrong kind of attention, but there was no problem with a little harmless dishonesty or mild trickery to get what you wanted.

Penny handed Tom the list, which he quickly scanned. 'What do you need all this for?' he asked, a slight frown on his face.

'Oh, nothing important. Just a couple of experiments that I want to run.' Otto had no intention of revealing the details of his plan to these two – they'd probably just think he'd gone quietly insane up here alone in the attic.

'OK,' Tom still didn't seem entirely satisfied with the answer he'd been given, 'but like Penny said, it could take a while.'

'A couple of days should be fine,' Otto replied, 'just make sure that you don't leave any tracks that can be followed back here.' His plan would only work if it came as a complete surprise. He couldn't afford any slip-ups. 'And if you manage to get everything on that list, there'll be a bonus in your allowances this week, a generous bonus.'

Tom and Penny both smiled at this.

'That would be nice,' Penny replied. 'We could do with a new TV in the girls' dormitory as well.'

'I'll see what I can do.' Otto smiled at her. 'The quicker you get me everything on that list, the bigger the television. How's that sound?'

Penny nodded at this, returning his smile. 'Seems fair. Come on Tom, we'd better get cracking.'

As the pair of them headed off down the stairs Otto

opened the paper again. There was the other headline that had caught his attention that morning:

PM PREPARES FOR
BRIGHTON PARTY CONFERENCE

The article went on to describe how many commentators felt that this would be the Prime Minister's toughest speech to the party yet. Otto stared at the accompanying photo of the PM looking stressed and tired as he left Number Ten.

'You don't know the meaning of tough yet, but you will . . . you will,' Otto said to himself as he stared at the photo.

☢☢☢

Within a few days Tom and Penny had been successful in their mission and returned with all of the supplies that Otto had requested. As usual they had been reluctant to discuss exactly how they had acquired some of the more exotic items on the list but Otto trusted that they would have been discreet. All he then had to do was actually start the process of assembling these components into the device that was central to his plan. He knew that the theory behind its design was sound, but he would still have to conduct some tests to ensure that it would work exactly as he intended. Despite all of this Otto felt strangely calm, as he always did when working on some new device or other.

Mrs McReedy, on the other hand, seemed to be going through the progressive stages of a nervous breakdown. Nothing that Otto said seemed to reassure her that the orphanage could be saved, and she seemed increasingly resigned to seeing the old place shut down. Otto guessed that she was just as nervous about auditors being brought in to analyse the orphanage's accounts and the embarrassing evidence that they might find of her improper use of the funds earmarked for Otto's private tuition.

The rumour mill had also been grinding away, and it seemed to Otto that one of his fellow orphans was stopping him in the corridor every five metres to see if there was any truth to the gossip that they'd been hearing. Otto knew better than to try and answer every one of these queries, knowing that if his scheme worked as planned none of them would have anything to worry about. Unfortunately his apparent indifference did little to calm the increasingly nervous atmosphere all around him.

Finally, with only a day to spare, Otto completed his work on the essential new device. He stood at a workbench in the attic busily packing a backpack with all of the supplies he'd need over the next couple of days.

There was a knock at the door and without looking up Otto shouted for the visitor to come in. Mrs McReedy entered.

'You wanted to see me, Otto?' She looked and sounded tired.

'Yes, Mrs McReedy, I just wanted to let you know that I'm going to be away for a couple of days. I have pressing business that I must attend to.' He continued packing his bag.

'Oh, Otto, do you have to go? With all that's going on at the moment I'm not sure that I can manage on my own.' She looked as if she might burst into tears again at any moment. Otto stopped packing his bag and walked over to Mrs McReedy. He placed a reassuring hand on her shoulder.

'Don't you worry, Mrs McReedy. It's only a couple of days and, if all goes according to plan, we won't have to worry about them trying to shut this old place down any more.' He gave her his most reassuring smile.

'So where are you going?' Mrs McReedy asked.

Otto grinned. 'To the seaside, Mrs McReedy. I'm going into politics.'

Chapter 6

The journey to the coast had proved uneventful. Otto had travelled down on the train and had checked into the hotel room that he had booked over the internet. It was a basic room but that hardly mattered given that he had no intention of spending the night there. He just needed somewhere private to set up his equipment for later in the day. Once he had set everything up and double checked that it was working properly, he set off down the seafront to reconnoitre the target.

Otto had found the conference centre with ease. The security was so tight that it would have been difficult to miss it. Otto had seen the commander of the security forces on the television a couple of days beforehand and he had boasted at great length about the 'ring of steel' that had been placed around the conference hall. He had claimed that it would be impossible for someone without the proper clearance to get anywhere near the conference and that he was entirely confident in the systems and procedures that they had put in place. This was, of course, like a red rag to a bull for Otto. He knew full well that the larger and more complicated the security operation the more likely it was that a tiny gap existed somewhere that he could exploit.

But Otto had no intention of actually trying to get into the building himself – he knew that would be next to impossible. No, he just needed to find a good place to leave the device and the rest should be easy. He strolled along the sea front, just outside the first ring of security checks, looking for the right spot. Then he saw it, a drain cover a couple of hundred yards from the conference centre that looked ideal. As he walked towards the drain he reached into his backpack and found the small pocket that contained the device. He pulled out a silver metallic sphere, about the size of a ping-pong ball, and smiled to himself. This was going to be too easy. He knelt down beside the drain cover, as if tying his shoe lace and, checking that no one was watching him, he dropped the ball down the drain. Slowly he retied the laces on his trainers, just in case anyone was watching. When he was satisfied that no one had seen what he'd done he stood up and headed back down the seafront, away from the conference venue. The Prime Minister's speech would start in about an hour. That would give him plenty of time to get back to his hotel room and get ready – the fun was about to begin.

☢ ☢ ☢

Otto checked there was nobody coming along the corridor of the hotel and then let himself into his room. He walked over and dumped his backpack on the bed, relieved to see that everything was exactly as he'd left it. He powered up his laptop computer which sat on the desk linked by a short length of cable to what looked like a tiny silver satellite dish. The machine started up and finally a window appeared with the two words **AWAITING DEPLOYMENT** flashing in its centre. Otto ran a couple of quick diagnostics and was pleased to see that the control interface to the device appeared to be working exactly as intended. He helped himself to a Coke from the minibar and settled down in front of the computer. Otto keyed in a new command and the status window changed, a new message appearing: **DEPLOYING AMBULATORY PROPULSION SYSTEM**.

Half a mile away along the seafront, in the bottom of the drain that Otto had found earlier, the sphere appeared to split in half, a gap a few millimetres wide appearing around its circumference. Eight tiny jointed metal limbs then slid out of the gap, twisting and locking into position, turning the sphere into something that looked like a cross between a pinball and a spider.

Back in his room Otto couldn't help but feel pleased with himself. The device was extremely complicated – he'd had to cram an enormous amount of technology into a tiny object – and yet everything appeared to be functioning properly. He had conducted tests in the attic at St Sebastian's, of course, but it was still a relief to see that the device was working as intended in the field. He issued a command and another window opened on his computer. This window showed a grainy picture of what the device could see, transmitted from a pinhole camera on its surface. Otto slowly rotated the device through all four points of the compass, trying to get a better idea of its immediate surroundings. He knew that the conference centre was a couple of hundred yards to the north-east of the drain, and he soon spotted a pipe that led away from the drain in that approximate direction. Pushing forward on the control stick attached to his computer, he sent the device scurrying down the pipe through the drains towards the conference centre, occasionally taking a pipe that branched off from the one that the device was currently in, trying to keep it on the correct course.

Otto spent several minutes manoeuvring the device carefully through the subterranean network of pipes and drains towards its destination. The layout of the system had seemed quite straightforward on the plans that Otto had acquired, but actually steering the right course through the murky maze of tunnels was proving to be slightly trickier than he had expected.

He was just starting to worry that he might have taken a wrong turn somewhere when he spotted his target. A faint light could be seen coming from a small opening up ahead, and Otto knew that this meant that he was in exactly the right place. He guided the device carefully through this new opening, the light getting stronger as it approached the gap at the far end of the path.

Otto pushed on the control stick again and the device started to climb the slippery walls of the pipe, heading up towards the opening.

'Incey, wincey spider climbed the waterspout . . . ' Otto sang softly to himself as the device approached the top of the pipe. He pushed another key and the pinhole camera extended out from the body of the sphere on a long flexible rod. Otto rotated the camera around, peeking out over the top of what he could now see was the plughole in a white-tiled shower cubicle. Thankfully the cubicle appeared to be empty and, retracting the camera again, he eased the spider up out of the plughole. He looked at the printouts of the conference centre's blueprints, which were spread out on the desk next to his computer. The plans had not been easy to get hold of, especially without arousing suspicion, and Otto suspected that they may even be slightly out of date but he hoped they would still serve his purposes adequately. Scanning the plans Otto realised that the device must have come up in the showers attached to the swimming pool changing rooms. The nearest access to the air conditioning system was in the changing room itself and so Otto sent the device scurrying across the shower cubicle floor, towards his target.

There were several men getting changed in the room and Otto tried hard not to look at their semi-naked, wobbly bodies as he steered the device through the shadows beneath the benches. He rotated the spider, using its camera to look around the walls for the vent cover that had to be there somewhere. He eventually spotted it high on the far wall – he would have to wait for the men in the room to finish getting changed. After what seemed like an eternity, but was probably only a couple of minutes, the men finished getting dressed and left the room, finally giving Otto his opportunity. The device would be exposed as it climbed the wall in order to reach the vent, so he'd have to move quickly. Pushing the control stick as far forward as it would go he sent the device dashing across the floor and up the wall towards the vent.

Suddenly the microphone on the device picked up the

sound of approaching voices. Someone was coming into the room! The tiny metallic spider still had a couple of feet to go before it reached the vent and it was climbing the smooth vertical surface of the wall as quickly as it could. Otto watched the vent getting larger and larger on his screen, willing the device to climb faster as it advanced inch by inch towards it. Otto rotated the camera to point back into the room and saw, to his horror, that two policemen had walked into the room, one of them holding a large dog on a leash that was sniffing the air in the room curiously. The microphone Otto had installed on the device picked up their conversation.

'We only checked in here a couple of hours ago. I can't believe he's making us repeat the search already,' one said to the other, looking fed up.

'Oh, you know what the chief's like,' the other replied. 'Everything by the book.'

Otto noticed that the dog was sniffing curiously around the door of the shower cubicle that the device had come up through. He couldn't understand it. The device shouldn't have any scent – it was just metal and plastic – so why should the dog be so interested in that particular cubicle? The dog turned, following the scent across the floor, tracking the precise trail that the device had followed. Suddenly it struck Otto. He was such an idiot, he told himself. The device itself might not smell of anything that the dog would be able to track, but he'd just sent it crawling several hundred yards through the drains and you could bet that would leave a scent trail that the animal would be able to trace.

The device had now reached the vent on the wall, and Otto very carefully manoeuvred its two front legs under the edge of the hinged grille, trying to lever open a space wide enough to squeeze itself through. He hoped that the hinge on the cover wouldn't be too stiff for the tiny machine to lift, and so was relieved to see that the gap that was being forced open was increasing steadily. He swivelled the camera again and saw the dog still sniffing the floor, advancing between the benches towards the vent with its handler in tow.

'Looks like Rex has got something here,' the handler remarked, kneeling down beside the dog. 'What you got, boy? Smell something? Go get it.' He unclipped the dog from its lead and it padded across the room, getting closer and closer to the device, which had almost finished dragging itself through the narrow gap at the base of the grille. Otto nudged the device forward again, and it finally pulled itself fully into the vent, its last leg vanishing through the gap. It was now fully inside the shaft, which sloped gently downwards into the darkness. Unfortunately, this tiny movement caught the dog's attention and it started to bark repeatedly, scraping at the wall with its front paws as it tried in vain to get closer to the vent by the ceiling.

The two policeman walked across the room towards the agitated dog, the man with the leash looked curiously at his canine companion.

'Well, he can definitely smell something up there. We'd better check that vent.'

Otto's blood ran cold. He edged the device away from the grille – if he could just get it a few more feet into the shaft he knew that the darkness would conceal it, but he only had a couple of seconds. Suddenly the face of one of the policemen appeared on the other side of the grille, peering curiously into the gloom within the shaft.

'I can't see much in there,' he informed his unseen colleague.

'You can open the grille. Look, it's just on a hinge,' replied the other policeman.

If he opened that grille, there was no way that he'd miss Otto's device sitting there. Equally, if Otto tried to move the device quickly the policeman would undoubtedly hear it walking on the metal-lined surface of the ventilation shaft. Otto thought frantically. Of course! He hit a key on his keyboard and the status window changed again, displaying **DEVICE DEACTIVATED**.

Within the air conditioning shaft the device's legs immediately retracted back into its spherical body and gravity did the rest. The sphere rolled silently away from the grate down the gently sloping shaft into the darkness, just as the policeman swung the grille upwards. Otto could still hear their voices as they checked the shaft.

'There's nothing in here. I don't know what Rex is getting so wound up about.'

'He probably just smelled something coming through the air conditioning from the kitchens. You know what he's like. Greedy old thing.'

The voices slowly faded away as the two policemen completed their search of the changing rooms and moved on. Back in his hotel room, Otto willed himself to relax, gradually feeling his heart rate slow. That had been too close, but he couldn't afford to lose his nerve now. He had about thirty minutes to get the device to its target position, and an unfamiliar system of ventilation shafts to navigate. There was no time to lose.

☹☹☹

The tiny mechanical spider skittered through the ventilation shafts on its spindly metal legs. Just round this corner, Otto thought to himself as he gently nudged the control stick, steering the device towards its target. The device rounded the corner and descended from the opening in the shaft into a small, dark space, just a couple of feet high. Otto knew that this area was actually

114

directly beneath the stage from which the Prime Minister would be making his speech in approximately five minutes' time. He rotated the device's camera, scanning its surroundings carefully, looking for his target. There it was, a few yards away – a bundle of cables dropping through a hole in the floor of the stage into the cramped space below. He manoeuvred the device so that it sat right next to the cables, quickly identifying the one he wanted. He pressed another key on his laptop:

INTERFACE MANDIBLES DEPLOYED, read the display.

Under the stage a pair of tiny metal pincers slid out from the device. Otto steered the pincers carefully towards the right cable and hit another key, making them clamp down hard on the wire.

INTERFACE ESTABLISHED, the display reported.

Otto ran a couple of quick diagnostics and was pleased to find that everything was working exactly as planned. OK, that's the hard part over with, Otto thought to himself, turning towards the television that sat on a table in the corner of his room. He thumbed the remote, turning the television on, and quickly flicked through the channels on offer. He soon found the one he wanted – a journalist talking to camera, while in the background was the stage under which Otto's device was secretly positioned. Otto sat waiting for a couple of minutes, half listening to the journalist pontificating on the importance of the speech for the Prime Minister. Otto also felt sure the Prime Minister would remember today as a pivotal moment in his career.

The journalist finished speaking just as the Prime Minister took the stage.

'Showtime,' Otto said softly to himself, turning back towards his computer.

Otto sat watching as the Prime Minister began his speech, not listening to what he was saying. He found politicians unspeakably boring and this speech was unlikely to be any exception. Let's give him a couple of minutes to get warmed up, he thought to himself.

He waited for a couple of minutes, the occasional stage-managed applause being the only break from the Prime Minister's interminable rambling. OK, enough, Otto thought to himself, and hit a key on the laptop. A window popped up, filled with slowly scrolling text. The words displayed were precisely the same as those being spoken by the Prime Minister, as this was a direct feed from his teleprompter. Between the blocks of text were instructions in brackets like (PAUSE FOR APPLAUSE) or (STRONG EMOTION). His finger hovering over the return key, Otto paused for a second, looking at the television.

'Goodbye, Prime Minister,' he said softly, bringing his finger down on the key.

It had taken Otto several days to perfect the program that was now running on his computer. Simply put, it transmitted a signal lasting no more than a couple of seconds directly to the angled glass screen of the Prime Minister's autocue. This wasn't any ordinary signal, though; it was designed to produce a very specific response. Otto knew that on the teleprompter screen on stage the text of the Prime Minister's speech had been replaced by a brief burst of white noise. The apparently random pattern of black and white pixels looked like a TV that was receiving no signal. But this was no random burst of static; this was a carefully calculated pattern that had taken Otto some time to perfect. This signal had the unique property of placing whoever viewed it immediately under Otto's total hypnotic control. He had already tested the program on Mrs McReedy, and after several minutes of her crawling around the floor on all fours barking like a dog he had been satisfied that it would work as intended. Conveniently, modern teleprompters were designed so that if they were viewed by anyone other than the speaker they looked like a clear sheet of angled glass, which meant that the only two people in the world who knew what had happened were Otto and the Prime Minister.

Otto glanced at the television and was pleased to see that the Prime Minister had stopped dead, in the middle of a sentence, and was now staring blankly at the tele-prompter. A few of the cabinet ministers seated behind him on the stage looked slightly confused, unsure what had silenced their leader like this. Amusing as it might be just to leave him standing there like a statue for a few minutes, Otto had other plans. He pressed another key on his computer and the hypnotic signal was replaced by more scrolling text. This wasn't the original speech, though – this was Otto's version.

The Prime Minister seemed to snap out of his trance and continued speaking as if nothing had happened.

'People of Britain, you are surely aware that I and the other members of my cabinet hold you and your families in nothing but the deepest contempt. Ruling over a bunch of drooling morons like you has been a ceaseless burden and, quite frankly, I don't think that we get enough credit for having to put up with your constant whining.' The Prime Minister's expression gave no hint that this new speech was in any way unusual. Behind him, his cabinet sat looking astonished, mouths hanging open in disbelief.

'The fact of the matter is that *we're* not public servants – you're our servants, you bunch of half-witted oiks, and the sooner you learn your proper place on your knees before us, the better. Let's face it – none of you have a fraction of the intelligence that we do,' he indicated the people sitting behind him, 'and half of you can barely read and write, and with the way the education system's going that's not going to change any time soon.'

There was now a general murmur of anger from the audience in the conference centre and a couple of the cabinet members were whispering urgently to one another. The Prime Minister continued, his familiar grin plastered across his face.

'So my message to you is really quite simple – we don't care. Never have done, never will do. You might as well shut your mouths and cut the moaning, because we don't give a monkey's. All that we care about is power and money; your dull, pathetic little problems are irrelevant.'

The Prime Minister's grin broadened.

'Quite frankly, you can take your problems and shove them. Thank you.'

Otto watched as the final instruction that would for ever destroy the Prime Minister's career in politics scrolled up the window on his computer.

(AS LONG AS YOU LIVE, YOU WILL NEVER TELL ANOTHER LIE)

The Prime Minister stood there grinning at the audience, clearly believing that he had given the speech of a lifetime, which Otto supposed was true, from a certain point of view. An evil idea suddenly formed in his head. He knew he shouldn't, but what the hell – when would he ever have another opportunity like this? Grinning, he typed one last command into the window.

(MOON THE AUDIENCE)

The Prime Minister dutifully turned around, bent over and dropped his trousers. The TV picture quickly changed from a shot of the PM's pale white bottom to one showing the horrified, open-mouthed expressions of the audience. Otto could no longer suppress a fit of giggles. Now that was an abject lesson in the true use of power.

He watched the television for a couple more minutes, amused by the bewildered reactions of the seasoned political journalists, who were desperately trying to make some kind of sense of what they had just seen. This one was going to run and run. Otto forced himself to turn back to his computer; it was time to cover his tracks. He typed a command into the machine and a window popped up.

SELF-DESTRUCT SEQUENCE INITIALISED

Beneath the stage the tiny silver spider dissolved into a pool of molten slag, leaving no identifiable trace of Otto's involvement. That was it – he was home and dry, and without the personal backing of the Prime Minister he doubted very much that the programme of orphanage closures would continue as planned. He felt uncharacteristically pleased with himself and as far as he was concerned he had every reason to. One of the journalists on the television caught his attention.

'August 29th, a date that will live in political infamy for ever . . .'

Was that the date? Otto had quite lost track of time while he'd been planning all of this. It was his birthday, or, more accurately, the anniversary of his arrival at St Sebastian's, which was the nearest thing he had to a proper birthday. Well, what better way to celebrate, he thought, toasting the Prime Minister with his can of Coke.

He watched the coverage of the unfolding political chaos for a few more minutes and then started to gather up his stuff and put it into his backpack. There was no reason now to stick around here any longer than he had to. Besides which, knowing Mrs McReedy there'd be a rather large birthday cake waiting for him back in London. The thought made him suddenly hungry.

Otto looked carefully around the room, making sure that he had left no trace of his activities that afternoon. Satisfied that the room was clean of evidence, he opened the door and cried out in surprise. Standing there in the doorway was a woman with short dark hair, dressed completely in black and with a curved scar on one cheek. All of these details, however, were secondary to the fact that she had a very large gun pointed directly at Otto's chest.

'Very impressive work today, Mr Malpense.' She had a slight foreign accent. 'But I'm afraid that playtime is over.' She raised the gun.

'I'm unarmed!' Otto blurted out. 'You're a police-woman, you can't shoot an unarmed child!' He raised his hands to emphasise his point.

She smiled in a way that made Otto's blood run cold. 'Who said I was from the police?'

Otto's eyes widened in horror.

ZAP!

Chapter 7

Otto awoke with a start. His Blackbox sat on his bedside table emitting an insistent bleeping sound. He picked up the device and flipped it open.

'Good morning, Mr Malpense,' said H.I.V.E.mind.

'Good morning, H.I.V.E.mind. What time is it?' Otto rubbed his eyes. He felt as if he'd only been asleep for five minutes.

'It is 7.30 a.m., Mr Malpense. Breakfast will be served in the dining room at 8 a.m. and lessons will commence at 9 a.m. May I be of any further assistance?' H.I.V.E.-mind enquired politely.

'No, not right now. Thank you, H.I.V.E.mind,' Otto replied and the Blackbox went dark as H.I.V.E.mind's glowing face disappeared.

Wing's Blackbox was sounding the same insistent alarm but it seemed to be having little effect on him. He slept on, his face calm, seemingly unaware of the increasingly loud noise coming from the device. Otto gently shook Wing's shoulder, trying to rouse him, and was astonished as Wing's hand shot from beneath the covers, pinning Otto's wrist in an uncomfortably firm grip. Wing blinked a couple of times and then, seeing that it was Otto, eased his vice-like hold.

'I'm sorry, Otto; I forgot where I was for a second.' Wing sat up in his bed. 'Or rather I had hoped it might all be some kind of bad dream. Unfortunately that does not appear to be the case.' He looked unhappily around their cramped new quarters.

'Yes, still here I'm afraid. I'm just going to have a quick shower. Breakfast's in half an hour.'

Otto and Wing quickly got showered and changed into their uniforms, new ones having been mysteriously delivered directly to their wardrobes during the night, just as Tahir had said they would be. Otto had placed a tiny mark on his uniform with a biro before he had put it away the previous night and now it was gone, meaning that this uniform had either been thoroughly cleaned or even, possibly, completely replaced. He made a mental note to check the wardrobe more thoroughly when they returned to the room.

They soon left their room and found that the atrium of accommodation area seven was filled with activity. What seemed like hundreds of students were making their way to breakfast, chatting and laughing, and Otto scanned the crowd looking for any familiar faces. After a couple of seconds he spotted Laura sitting in an armchair, looking slightly overwhelmed by the commotion all around her.

'Look, there's Laura.' Otto pointed her out to Wing. 'Come on, let's go and say good morning.'

Laura gave the two boys a broad smile as they approached.

'Good night's sleep?' she enquired, still smiling.

'For Wing, certainly,' Otto replied, 'though possibly not anyone within a hundred yards of him. If whales snore, that's what it sounds like.'

Wing smiled guiltily. 'I did warn you.'

'It's a sign of a good healthy set of lungs, at least that's what my dad always used to tell me,' Laura said, chuckling, 'though I think there were a few nights where my mum was not far from taking a kitchen knife and checking to see if his were as healthy as he claimed, if you know what I mean.'

Otto nodded in agreement. 'I wonder if you snore after you get hit with a sleeper?'

'Don't even think about it,' Wing replied.

The three of them sat watching as the other students who lived in this accommodation area continued to mill around the atrium. A few were already heading off to the dining hall, obviously keen to avoid the inevitable queues.

'So, who are you sharing with?' Otto asked Laura.

'Shelby,' she said, sounding rather exasperated. 'She's still up in the room, getting ready. I was only allowed to use the bathroom for five minutes because half an hour is apparently barely enough time for her to get ready properly. At least that's what she's told me about twenty times since she woke up.'

Otto laughed. 'Just wait till she finds out that H.I.V.E. doesn't have a beauty salon, then there'll be hell to pay.'

Wing had spotted something over Otto's shoulder. 'Look, there's Nigel and Franz.'

Otto knew that the two boys had been assigned a room together and he wondered how their first night sharing had gone. Both of them were still wearing the same looks of bemused nervousness that they seemed to have had all day yesterday. Eventually, the German boy looked over towards where Otto, Wing and Laura were sitting and waved to them, nudging Nigel and pointing over in their direction. Otto waved back, gesturing for the two boys to join them.

'I hope you are all having a nice sleep?' Franz ventured as he and Nigel sat down.

'Yes, fine thanks. You?' Laura replied.

'Ja, I am being able to sleep, despite my great hunger.' Franz gave them a serious look, obviously keen to stress the great hardship he was enduring. 'Have any of you seen a snack machine?'

Nigel sighed. 'Franz, we're going to breakfast in ten minutes, what do you need a snack machine for?'

'To be building up my energy levels for a long day of lessons, of course.' Franz gave Nigel a slap on the back that, judging by Nigel's pained expression, was a little overenthusiastic. 'And you will be needing building up too, my friend. Do not worry, Franz will turn you into a real man.' Otto noted the slightly frightened look on Nigel's face and guessed that he was less than keen to be the first person to try the Argentblum Diet.

'Anyway, why have vending machines when none of us have any money?' Otto asked. The apparent lack of any form of currency on H.I.V.E. was something that Otto had actually given a lot of thought. He had finally reached the conclusion that if money truly was the root of all evil it might just be adding fuel to the fire to introduce the concept to H.I.V.E.

'Ja, I have been thinking this too but I am hoping that the machines will be free of charge. That would be seeming sensible, ja?'

Otto doubted very much that the words 'free snack food vending machines' and 'sensible' should ever be used in the same sentence where Franz was concerned.

'Well, I'm afraid I didn't see any yesterday on the tour, and there don't seem to be any around here, so we may have to do without crisps and chocolate,' Laura observed.

'Truly this is a place of evil.' Franz looked dejected.

Otto checked the time on his Blackbox. 'Come on, breakfast starts soon. We'd better get going.'

The five of them headed towards the exit and were just about to leave the atrium when they heard a shout behind them. It was Shelby.

'Hey, wait for me you guys!' she shouted, hurrying to catch up with them. Clearly she had managed to make good use of the limited time that she'd had to get ready. She somehow looked more awake than the rest of them, not a single hair out of place. Otto also couldn't help but notice that Laura looked less than delighted at Shelby's arrival, and he wondered if there had already been some kind of argument between them.

'Come on, Shelby, you're going to make us late,' Laura said impatiently.

'It's not my fault that they don't give you enough time to get ready in the morning; I had to completely skip my aura cleansing.' Shelby looked genuinely indignant at this outrageous state of affairs.

'Well, I'm sure you'll manage somehow.' Laura replied sharply.

Yes, thought Otto as they all headed towards the exit, definitely some tension there.

☢ ☢ ☢

They arrived five minutes early for their first lesson, Villainy Studies, and were now sitting at their desks, waiting for the arrival of Dr Nero. Otto was keen to see what this first lesson would be like. It would, at least, afford him the opportunity to study Dr Nero a little more closely, which he was sure would prove useful. It was Sun Tzu who had taught him that the key to victory was to know your enemy, and he intended to learn all he could about the mysterious Doctor.

Wing sat next to him, flicking through the pages of the textbook that they would need for this lesson, *Elementary Evil*.

'Have you read any of this?' Wing asked, looking slightly worried.

'No,' Otto lied. He had in fact read the entire book the previous evening. It had only taken him a couple of minutes but he didn't want anyone to know about his sponge-like ability to absorb information yet. 'Anything interesting?' he enquired.

'I'm not sure interesting is the right word,' Wing replied, 'more like astonishing and slightly frightening. I am keen to see what light Dr Nero can throw on the subject.' He frowned.

Otto knew what Wing meant. The book seemed to suggest that evil was a job like any other and not a philosophical concept at all. It offered page after page of advice and practical examples of how the reader could improve their evil performance, helping them climb the career ladder of wickedness more quickly. Otto suspected that there couldn't be many other books in the world with chapter titles like 'Eliminating the Opposition', 'No Pain, No Reign' and 'Diabolical Performance Analysis'.

Suddenly the classroom door opened and the room fell silent as Dr Nero walked in and made his way over to the desk at the front of the room.

'Good morning, students. I hope that you have all settled into your new quarters without any problems.' Nero moved around the desk and slowly scanned the faces of the nervous-looking students. 'You all know my name, but I'm afraid I don't know all of yours yet so if I make any mistakes please bear with me.

'The name of this class is Villainy Studies, and it is in these lessons that you will learn to embrace your true potential, to unlock the true villain that lurks inside each and every one of you. It is, however, important to make one thing very clear from the start. I am not interested in training you to be common criminals – six months in any typical prison would achieve that. Instead I will teach you to aspire to loftier goals, to push yourself further than you might previously have thought you could go. H.I.V.E. does not train bank robbers, burglars, car thieves, or muggers. In short, we will not teach you to be petty crooks. Nor do we advocate mindless violence – except of course in the Henchman stream – a true villain should not have to dirty their hands with such things. You won't blackmail individuals, you'll blackmail governments. You won't rob banks, you'll take them over. You won't kidnap people, you'll steal aircraft carriers.

'Now I know what at least some of you will be thinking. Isn't this evil? Isn't this wrong? Well, let me answer that for you.' Nero paused, as if trying to spot those in the room who might harbour these doubts.

'Evil,' he continued, 'is a woefully misunderstood concept. Most ordinary people would define evil using words like "bad" or "wrong", but it is my intention to show you that its real meaning is much deeper and more complex than that. These might be the definitions that ordinary people choose, but you are not like them – you are extra-ordinary, and as such you do not need to live your lives within the suffocating restraints of their moral codes. You are all capable of evil – everyone is – but the real challenge before you now is to understand that evil does not mean wrong. Evil must have purpose, a determination to get what you want by any means necessary, strength in the face of adversity, intelligence in a world ruled by stupidity. You are the leaders of tomorrow, men and women who can, and will, change the face of this planet for ever.'

Thermonuclear weapons could change the face of the

planet for ever, Otto thought; it didn't mean to say that they should be viewed as role models for the ambitious go-getter.

Nero continued, 'I'm sure that there must have been times when you have read books or watched films and found yourself secretly wishing for the villain to win. Why? Isn't that against the rules by which our society lives? Why should you feel this way? It's simple really; the villain is the true hero of these tales, not the well-intentioned moron who somehow foils their diabolical scheme. The villain gets all the best lines, has the best costumes, has unlimited power and wealth – why on earth would anyone NOT want to be the villain? But you see, that's the real problem. If the masses realised how much more fun life would be if they could all wear the black costume, where would that leave us? What would become of society if people understood that in the real world the hero rarely wins against overwhelming odds and that the villain always has the last laugh? The world would be locked in a perpetual state of anarchy, in all likelihood. So it is important that such an education only be given to those who deserve it, those who have the intelligence and strength of character to understand the power that they wield. Let the masses have their fantasy heroes, and meanwhile the best of what the world has to offer will be yours for the taking.'

Otto had no doubt that Nero had given this speech many times before. It had the ring of a well-practised hard-sell routine. That wasn't to say it didn't work. The class sat quietly, listening intently to what Nero was saying. A couple of the students were even taking notes, much to Otto's amusement. The way that Nero described it, embracing life as a villain was an opportunity not to be missed.

'Of course the best way to learn anything is to study the masters of your chosen craft at work, and so we will examine the greatest villains throughout history in an attempt to better understand what it is that distinguishes the true evil genius from the gifted sociopath. Throughout history there have been men and women who have demonstrated that villainy is not just a job but an art form, and these people shall be your role models, your heroes, the examples that you should seek to follow.'

Nero looked around the room again – he made a point of ensuring that he taught this particular course to the new Alpha students each year. It was always a delicate balancing act making sure that the school produced leaders and not monsters. Each and every child in this room had the potential to be either and it was his job, as the head of the school, to ensure that H.I.V.E. did not unleash any pupil on the world who would tip the delicate balance of world power towards anarchy. Creating such chaos, attractive as it might be to some, was not at all the type of thing that Nero wanted from his pupils, they had to learn the importance of discretion and style in this new line of work.

'With this in mind I intend to start today by looking at the illustrious career of one of our past alumni, the now sadly departed Diabolus Darkdoom.' Nero picked up a small remote control from the desk and thumbed a button. A screen slowly lowered from the ceiling behind him, showing a picture of a strikingly handsome man. He wore a long black frock coat and held a duelling sword, its tip resting on the ground. His head was completely bald and his calm expression seemed to convey a sense of self-confidence and capability.

Otto glanced over at Nigel, who did not look happy that his father was going to be the topic of that day's lesson. Nero had to be aware of the fact that Nigel was Diabolus's son, and it seemed that he was deliberately choosing, for whatever reason, to put him in this uncomfortable situation.

'As some of you may already know,' Nero walked over and placed a hand on Nigel's shoulder, 'a member of the Darkdoom family is actually here with us today, and I would like to start by saying that I'm sure we all wish to pass on our condolences on the recent loss of your father, Nigel.'

Nigel seemed to shrink slightly in his seat as he became the focus of attention of everyone in the room.

'Thank you,' he mumbled, his pale face turning slowly crimson.

'For those of you who don't know, Nigel's father was one of the greatest villains the world has ever known. His exploits upon graduating from H.I.V.E. have become the stuff of legend, and I can think of no better role model for you all to adopt over the coming years.'

Apart from the dying prematurely part, Otto hoped.

'To truly understand what it was that made Diabolus such an exceptional example, we must look more closely at his history and the details of some of his more famous schemes. One of the best examples was when he succeeded in kidnapping the American president a few years ago and replacing him with an android replica. It took nearly three weeks for anyone to notice . . .'

For the next hour Nero continued to chronicle Darkdoom Senior's life, detailing one nefarious plot after another, each one seemingly more devilishly cunning than the last one. It was quite unlike any history lesson that Otto had previously experienced – Nero was giving them a glimpse of a world that the majority of the planet's population weren't even aware existed. This was a world where the massed legions of villainy were engaged in a never-ending struggle with the forces of justice that was kept entirely secret from everyone else. Otto couldn't help but be astonished by some of the events that had taken place right under the unsuspecting noses of the general public. But, thanks to a suspiciously convenient lack of coverage by the media and some gargantuan cover-ups by national governments, the vast majority of people remained blissfully unaware of this clandestine war that was going on around them.

Otto kept a close eye on Nigel throughout this exploration of his father's life. There would be an occasional look of astonishment on his face as Nero would detail some event or plot that his father had been responsible for that suggested that there were things that even his son hadn't known about him.

As the end of the lesson drew near, Nero invited them to ask questions about what they had seen. Multiple hands shot up around the room and Nero pointed at a boy with curly blond hair at the back of the room.

'Yes, Mr Langstrom. What would you like to ask?'

'What happened to Darkdoom?' the boy asked.

'Well, you will understand, I'm sure, if I don't want to go into detail concerning that, out of respect for Nigel's feelings. You must remember that these events, while of historical interest to you, are still painfully recent memories for him,' Nero replied.

Otto was glad that Nigel would be spared the details of his father's death, but he couldn't help feeling curious himself. From the way that Diabolus had been described it was hard to imagine a situation that would lead to his demise. Judging from the pained expression on Nigel's face it was likely that he knew exactly what had happened to his father and that it was not a pleasant memory.

The boy nodded. 'Yes, of course. Sorry, I wasn't thinking.' Nigel looked relieved that the subject was not going to be discussed in detail.

Nero picked out another raised hand, inviting a girl with her hair in dreadlocks to speak.

'It seems like some of the elements of his schemes were pointless. Why build a fully manned space station with an orbital laser cannon mounted on it when it would have been easier to just put the laser into orbit and control it from the ground, or even just destroy his targets with conventional weapons? Why risk detection by going to all that trouble? It's not like all that extra effort made his plan any more effective.'

Nero smiled. 'A very good question, and one whose answer lies at the very core of what we hope to teach you at H.I.V.E. What Diabolus understood, and what I hope you will all come to understand as well, is that a scheme must have style; a plot must have a plot, if you will. There are people all over the world who have the talent and the ability to put together a simple criminal scheme, but we must always strive to elevate ourselves beyond that level. Is it necessary to build a giant robotic squid to destroy shipping? Why not just use torpedoes or sabotage? Because it's been done before. When you graduate from H.I.V.E. you will be the trailblazers, the cutting edge of evil, leaders for whom the conventional should never be good enough. As such your schemes should never rely on what has been done before – they must be original, cunning and, above all, stylish. Let the common criminal follow awestruck in your footsteps while you push ahead, searching for the next challenge, always innovating, never standing still.'

Otto noticed that many of the students in the room seemed slightly confused by this, but it made perfect sense to him. It was as if Nero was describing something that Otto had always been aware of, this need to not only win but to win with style. He couldn't deny that it sounded attractive, and for the first time since he had arrived on the island he found himself wondering if there really was something that H.I.V.E. had to offer him.

MWAH, MWAAAAH, MWAH!!!!

The school bell rang to signal the end of the lesson, making Otto jump. Nero raised his voice as the children began to pack their books and notes away.

'For next week's lesson I want you all to have studied the first three chapters of *Elementary Evil*. There will be a short test and I expect you all to get full marks. Class dismissed.'

Chapter 8

Otto and Wing made their way through the bustling corridors, heading for the Tactical Education department and their first lesson with Colonel Francisco. Franz and Nigel were walking just ahead of them, Franz chatting animatedly to a subdued-looking Nigel.

'Do you think Nigel is all right?' Wing asked, looking with concern at the short, bald boy.

'I don't think that he was quite prepared to go through his father's life story in his very first lesson, if that's what you mean,' Otto replied.

'Diabolus cannot have been the only person that was worthy of study,' Wing noted. 'One has to wonder why Dr Nero chose such an emotive subject.'

'You'll go mad trying to second guess that man. Whatever his reasons, it can't have been easy for Nigel.' Otto looked again at Nigel, who seemed to be lost in thought despite Franz's constant chatter. Otto picked up his pace. 'Come on, let's rescue him from Franz.'

'Hi guys,' Otto greeted them. 'So, have either of you heard anything about this Colonel Francisco that we ought to know?'

'Ja, I am hearing from one of the other students that he is being one of the toughest teachers at the school,' Franz replied, looking slightly nervous. Otto reckoned that Franz's nerves might have more to do with the prospect of imminent physical exertion that anything else.

'Well, that's good to know, considering what pussy cats all of the other teachers we've met so far have been,' Otto replied sarcastically. 'What about you, Nigel? Have you heard anything interesting about him?'

'No, not really.' Nigel sounded thoroughly depressed. He didn't seem to be able to look the others in the eye. 'But I bet he's heard of my dad.' There was a surprising bitterness in his voice.

'Ja, your father was being the big cheese around here, I think,' Franz replied cheerily, seemingly oblivious to Nigel's apparent unhappiness.

'Well, I just wish everyone would shut up about him.' Nigel seemed genuinely angry for a moment before his previous glumness returned. 'I'm sick of hearing about how bloody wonderful he was. You didn't have to live with him.'

Nero sat at his desk in his study, impatiently waiting for the video screen on the opposite wall to flicker into life. He was scheduled to receive a call from Number One, the only man in the world he found intimidating, the commander of the Global League of Villainous Enterprises, or G.L.O.V.E. Very little was actually known about the man other than the fact that over the last forty years he had built G.L.O.V.E up from a small criminal cartel to the most powerful and widespread syndicate that the world had ever known. Nobody knew his true identity – he made a point of never meeting with anyone in person – and there were a thousand different theories as to who he might actually be. The fact remained that the only people who had ever tried to usurp him had been dealt with swiftly and brutally, serving as a powerful example to any others who might secretly harbour such plans.

As usual the call had been pre-arranged by Number One's subordinates, and Nero was expected to be in a position to receive the call at the appointed time. Woe betide the man who was not dutifully sitting waiting when Number One called – he was not known for his patience. And so it was that Nero sat watching the second hand of the clock on his desk slowly sweep around to the appointed time. He had never known a call from Number One to even be a second late and he doubted very much that this would be the first time.

As the second hand ticked past twelve the video screen lit up with the familiar H.I.V.E. fist and globe logo. The symbol faded away to be replaced by a silhouette of a man, his appearance entirely hidden.

'Maximilian. It is good to speak with you again,' the shadowy figure on the screen began.

'The honour is mine, Number One. There is something that you wished to discuss with me?' Nero asked.

'Indeed. I trust that the latest intake of students has been successfully acquired.'

'Yes, sir. This year's intake numbered nearly two hundred students across all streams, our highest new intake for some time.'

'And the retrieval operations went smoothly?'

Nero contemplated telling Number One about the difficulties that the retrieval team had when trying to recruit the Fanchu boy, but decided against it. He knew that there was a chance that Number One may have already heard about the incident – he did after all appear to have sources of intelligence in every corner of the globe – but he trusted his operatives' discretion in such matters.

'No, Number One. Everything proceeded according to plan,' Nero replied, keeping his voice even. Number One was notorious for his ability to sense a lie.

'Good. I would be most disappointed if anything happened to reveal any hint of H.I.V.E.'s existence to the world. We cannot afford to relocate the school again.'

'Our existence is still a secret, sir, you can rest assured of that.' Nero knew what the personal consequences would be if this ever ceased to be the case.

'Good. See that it remains that way,' Number One replied.

Nero knew that Number One was not just calling to discuss the retrieval of the new intake of students. He had already detailed the success of the operation in his usual report to G.L.O.V.E. and Number One could easily have found that information within it.

'Is there anything else, Number One?' Nero enquired, knowing that there must be.

'Yes, there is one other thing. The Malpense child.'

Alarm bells started to ring in Nero's head.

'Yes, sir, he arrived safely yesterday.'

'Yes, I know. You may be curious to know who is sponsoring his admission to the program.'

Nero was indeed curious. He had checked Malpense's records after he had greeted the new students in the entrance cavern. The Contessa's report on his behaviour during the introductory tour and the incident in the dining hall had only confirmed Nero's initial impression of the boy, and he had been keen to find out as much as possible about this new student. After all, it was not every day that H.I.V.E. took in a new student who had already deposed a head of state before they had even started their training. Nero had become more curious when he had tried to access the details of Otto's sponsor, only to be informed that his G.L.O.V.E. security clearance was not high enough to access that information. This had astonished and then worried Nero. It had certainly never happened before, and there were very few people in the world who had a higher security clearance than he did.

'Yes, sir. It is somewhat irregular that I cannot access the details of his sponsor, though I'm sure it was for a very good reason.' Nero picked his words carefully; talking with this man could be like tap dancing in a minefield.

'Yes, there is a good reason, and it is something that you at least should be aware of. I am sponsoring the Malpense child personally.'

Nero felt a sudden chill. Number One had never sponsored a student at the school before.

'I see. Is there any particular reason why you have chosen to sponsor him? I mean, is there anything I should know that might help with his future education?'

'My reasons are my own. I would have thought that you would know better than to question them by now, Maximilian.' Number One's voice seemed to harden for a second, and Nero felt the hairs on the back of his neck prickle.

'Of course, sir. I did not mean to question your decision, I'm sure that he will prove to be an excellent student.' Nero struggled to suppress the anxious note in his voice.

'As am I. I will expect regular reports on his progress.'

'Of course, sir. Is there anything else?'

'See that no harm comes to him, Nero. Doubtless he will suffer occasional injuries as part of his training, but no serious harm must befall him. I am holding you personally responsible for his safety.'

'Very well, Number One. Is there anything else?'

'No, that is all. Pass on my best wishes to your staff.'

To remind them that he was always watching, Nero thought to himself.

'I will, Number One.'

'I shall speak to you again soon, Maximilian. Good-bye.'

The video screen went dark. Nero sat back in his chair, trying to make sense of what Number One had just told him. He had never sponsored a child at the school before, so there was clearly something about Malpense that had changed his mind, and Nero had to find out what it was. In the meantime he would have to instruct Raven not only to keep an eye on the boy but also to make sure that nothing untoward happened to him. Her talents were not normally used to protect students, but he had little doubt that she would make the best and most discreet bodyguard for the boy. It would not do for the staff or students to become aware of the special treatment Malpense was receiving so she would have to remain as invisible as possible. Fortunately, as her past victims would attest, there were very few people who saw Raven until it was far too late to do anything about it.

Nero pulled up Otto's records on the computer on his desk and scanned the details again, looking for some piece of information that he had missed that might give him some clue as to Number One's motivations for choosing the boy. There was nothing immediately obvious, other than the audacity of his last scheme, but Nero resolved to find out as much as he could about Otto Malpense. His own survival might depend upon it.

Chapter 9

The Tactical Education department was almost like a school within a school. As Otto made his way towards the cavern where their first lesson with Colonel Francisco was due to take place he saw classrooms, firing ranges, gyms, climbing walls, swimming pools and a host of other facilities that appeared to be unique to this department. He also noticed that there were many more henchman students in this area than he had seen before, the vast majority of whom seemed to have the same imposing build as Block and Tackle. Otto saw that Wing was constantly surveying their surroundings with a practised eye, as if expecting to be ambushed at any moment. Otto supposed that he too was looking out for any sign of their lunchtime sparring partners from the previous day.

The atmosphere in this department was quite different to any other part of the school that the new Alpha students had seen so far. There was a feeling of barely suppressed aggression that seemed to pervade the entire area, and this was only made more intimidating by the openly hostile glares that they received from the blue-overalled thugs that surrounded them. It was with some relief that they finally arrived at the entrance to the correct cavern, the heavy steel doors rumbling apart to admit them.

They walked through the door and on to a large metal platform that was suspended from the wall of a deep cavern, a pool of dark water filling its base far below. Hanging down from the roof of the cavern, level with the platform, was a bizarre arrangement of girders and concrete blocks, looking almost like a suspended assault course. Standing at the far side of the platform was the enormous black man in military uniform whom Otto had spotted on the teachers' table at lunch the previous day. He was wearing the same military-style camouflage fatigues and heavy black boots polished to a high shine, and looked thoroughly formidable. Now that Otto could observe him more closely he could also see that what he had taken to be some kind of gauntlet that the man wore was in fact a fully articulated artificial metal hand, suggesting that handshakes should probably be avoided if one wanted to avoid an unscheduled trip to the infirmary. He looked like the sort of person who would happily rip the head off anyone who did not do exactly as he instructed. As the last of the Alphas passed through the doors he bellowed at the group.

'Right! Listen up, you worthless bunch of maggots. I am Colonel Francisco, but that's "sir" to you. You will obey my orders at all times immediately and without question. If any of you disobey my orders, I will personally see to it that the next few years are a living hell for you – that's a promise. I doubt that I'll be able to do much with a bunch of no-good Alphas like you, but let's see what you've got. Form up!'

He pointed to the circles painted on the floor in front of him and each of the students hurriedly took up position on one of the marks.

'Stand to attention, now! Feet together, eyes forward!' Francisco screamed at them, and they hurriedly obeyed. 'What a pitiful display of spineless specimens,' the Colonel said, walking along the line of students. 'This is the first stage of your Tactical Education programme. It is highly unlikely that any of you will display even the tiniest bit of natural ability for what I will be trying to teach you, but I will not tolerate quitters. You give your all or I will damn well take it from you. Do I make myself clear?'

There were a few mumbles of agreement from the group, most of whom appeared to be in a state of mild shock.

'I can't hear you! When I ask you a question you will answer loud and clear. The first and last words I want to hear from each and every one of you is "sir."

Is that clear?' He glared at them, as if daring them to defy him.

'Sir, yes sir!' the group replied loudly in unison.

'Good. I intend to start your training by familiarising you with one of the most basic and fundamental pieces of equipment that you will use during your time at H.I.V.E.' He walked over to a rack of strange black objects and picked one up. It looked like an armoured gauntlet with a small handle at one end and a bulky assembly attached to one side with a silver arrowhead protruding from it.

'This is a mark-four tactical grappler unit,' the Colonel barked, slipping the device on to his arm. 'You will all become familiar with every aspect of its operation and tactical use. It is not a complicated piece of equipment, so even you Alphas should be able to understand it.'

Otto was beginning to get an idea where the hostility that the henchmen exhibited towards the Alpha students came from.

'The primary trigger is located on the handle here.' He pointed to the handgrip. 'This will fire the grappling line, like so.' He pointed the device straight up at the ceiling of the cavern and pressed the button. There was a small popping sound and a steel bolt, trailing a thin wire, shot from the barrel of the device and straight into the rock above. 'The secondary switch is located under your thumb, and is used to reel the line in and out.' There was a slight whining noise from the device and the Colonel was pulled several feet into the air, hanging suspended before them. After dangling there for a second he pushed the switch in the opposite direction and lowered himself on to the platform again.

'Pull the trigger for a second time to release the grappler.' As he pressed the button the bolt released from the ceiling above and, with another high-pitched whine, the line reeled back into the unit at lightning speed, the pointed bolt snapping into place.

'Individually these devices can be used to scale vertical surfaces or to descend safely from elevated positions, but a pair of grapplers can be more useful.' The Colonel walked back over to the rack and took a second grappler, snapping it on to his other arm. He stepped to the edge of the platform and fired a line towards the strange obstacles suspended from the roof. The bolt struck a concrete block and attached itself firmly.

'Watch closely. You will all be expected to try this shortly.' With that the Colonel stepped off the platform and swung out towards the centre of the cavern. As he reached the apex of his swing he released the line and started to drop, drawing gasps from a couple of the watching students. As he fell he fired the second grappler, the bolt fixing firmly to a distant block. He stopped falling, swinging now at great speed towards the other side of the cavern. He continued to swing from arm to arm, seeming to miss some of the obstacles by just a few centimetres, but always maintaining a constant speed. He moved with surprising grace and agility for a man of his size and had soon cleared the field of obstacles. When he approached the far side of the cavern he turned round and swung back again, switching from line to line just in time to avoid seemingly inevitable collisions. Finally he landed softly on the platform in front of the assembled students. He didn't even appear to be out of breath. It had been an impressive display.

'As you will have noticed, when used in this way a pair of grapplers can be used to transport you at high speed through an elevated environment. It will take considerable practice for you to achieve a basic level of competence with this equipment and with that in mind I want each of you to take a pair of grappler units and attempt to traverse the cavern to the platform on the opposite wall.' The Colonel pointed across the cavern, indicating an identical platform that was partially obscured by the intervening obstacles. The students all looked suitably apprehensive at having to make the crossing, warily eyeing the drop to the dark water below.

Franz raised his hand nervously.

'Yes!' the Colonel barked, making Franz jump.

'This is seeming rather dangerous. What if we fall?' Franz asked, glancing again at the water below.

The Colonel stalked over to where Franz was standing and bent down towards him.

'Do I look like someone that would place you in a dangerous situation?' he growled, his nose inches from Franz's.

Franz looked like a rabbit caught in headlights. This was clearly a question for which there was no correct answer.

'Um . . . yes.' Franz chose the answer that seemed least likely to bring about his imminent demise.

'Good, because that's exactly what I am, and you just volunteered to go first, maggot,' said the Colonel with an evil smile. Franz looked horrified, but clearly realised that there was little point arguing with the Colonel, and he walked over to the rack of grapplers with the look of a condemned man. The Colonel quickly chose a pair of grapplers for Franz and put them on his arms, pointing out to the others how they should be fastened properly.

'Right, let's see what you've got,' the Colonel said, gesturing for Franz to take up a position at the edge of the platform. Franz stood there, looking down over the edge with an expression of terror.

'I am hoping this water is deep,' he muttered to himself, slowly raising his arm to point the grappler at a point on the ceiling some distance away. He pressed one of the buttons and the bolt shot through the air, fixing to the ceiling with a thunk. He looked down again and then over his shoulder at the Colonel.

'I am thinking that I cannot do this,' he said nervously, his face white.

'Only one way to find out, maggot,' the Colonel replied, and shoved Franz hard in the back, sending him falling forwards off the platform.

'Aaaaarrrrrrggggghh!!' Franz screamed as he swung out from the platform. He spun and twisted, looking for all the world like a fish hooked on the end of a line. While the Colonel's demonstration had been a display of grace and agility, Franz's first attempt was more like a drunken wrecking ball. In his panic Franz had not even tried to fire off a second line, and after a few seconds he was left dangling at the end of the vertical wire, spinning gently, his eyes firmly closed. The Colonel did not look happy.

'Fire the second line, you useless sack of lard!!' he bellowed at the stranded Franz. 'Or you'll be hanging there all day!'

Franz raised his free arm obediently, one eye still closed, and fired the second grappler randomly at where he hoped the ceiling might be. The second bolt shot out, trailing its line, and secured itself to one of the concrete blocks dangling from the ceiling, leaving Franz hanging suspended from the two lines.

'Now release the first line,' the Colonel instructed. Franz

did as he was told and swung out again, towards the middle of the cavern. This process continued for several minutes, and despite the Colonel's barked instructions Franz only proceeded slowly towards the other platform, stopping and dangling between each swing. With his final swing Franz released the line prematurely and fell several feet on to the metal platform, landing in an undignified heap.

'Right, who's next?' The Colonel slowly surveyed the group, choosing the next victim. 'You'll do,' he snarled, pointing at Shelby. 'Let's see if you can do any better than our first volunteer.'

'Sure, no problem,' she replied. Shelby did not appear to be overly concerned at the prospect of trying to make it across the cavern. She calmly walked over to the rack, fastened a grappler on to each arm and approached the edge of the platform. She turned when she reached the drop-off and winked at the Colonel before swan-diving off the platform without even firing off her first line. The gathered group gave a collective gasp as Shelby disappeared. A split second later a line shot up from beneath the platform and she swung out towards the centre of the cavern like a rocket. She appeared totally relaxed – there was no hint of the panicked twisting that had made Franz's attempt so painfully slow. Instead, Shelby appeared completely at home with the challenge, releasing one line moments before firing the other, using the speed

155

gained in each short drop to make each successive swing faster and faster. She shot between the obstacles between the two platforms, seeming to miss collisions by just millimetres on several occasions, finally landing on the other side as lightly as a feather. It was hard to tell who was more astonished by this display, the students or the Colonel, whose mouth was hanging open in surprise.

'Good . . . er . . . yes. That's how it should be done. Yes, very good.' The Colonel had clearly never seen anyone make their first crossing of the cavern quite like that before. Otto nudged Wing, raising a single eyebrow at him. It did not surprise Otto that there was more to Shelby than the grating personality she projected – he had already guessed that she was keeping something about her past secret. He just had to find out what that secret was.

Over the course of the next half hour the rest of the class attempted the crossing. Several had obviously had their confidence boosted by Shelby's display, but found that the exercise was rather more difficult than it looked. This led to more than one of the students making the rather humiliating, not to mention soggy, ascent of the ladder that led up from the water at the bottom of the cavern to the platform. Nigel was one of these unfortunate few after swinging face-first into one of the concrete blocks in the centre of the cavern. The crunching impact drew a sympathetic 'Ooohh' from the watching crowd. He now stood dripping on the platform, looking thoroughly miserable, sporting what promised to be an impressive bruise on his cheekbone.

Otto was not terribly surprised when Wing crossed over quickly and efficiently, seeming quite at home with this deranged trapeze act. He didn't look as comfortable as Shelby as he swung across the cavern, but nor did it appear to present him with any real problems. Otto was quite apprehensive about having to make the crossing himself, but once he started his first swing he found it surprisingly easy. He had never been the most physically active person, but as he swung through the air he found the whole process strangely instinctive. It was almost as if he could see his trajectory mapped out in the air ahead of him – this was, after all, just physics, he reminded himself, and he was little more than a glorified pendulum. He may have lacked some of the flair of Shelby or Wing, but he made it safely to the other side without joining the ranks of the unsuccessful students, who were now each standing in the middle of their own small puddles.

The Colonel stood in front of the group, a look of mild disgust on his face.

'With very few exceptions you have performed predictably terribly today. Hardly surprising for Alphas.' He stalked along the line of students and stopped in front of

Shelby, jabbing his finger at her. 'What's your name, maggot?' he asked bluntly.

'Shelby Trinity, sir,' she replied.

'You look like you've done this before, Trinity,' he said, looking at her closely.

'No, sir. Just beginner's luck, sir,' Shelby replied, a tiny smile flickering across her mouth for an instant.

'If that's true, you're the luckiest beginner I've ever encountered. Your performance was acceptable. Keep it up.'

Otto knew that this was something of an understatement. Her performance had been just as good as the Colonel's, and this had apparently been her first attempt. The Colonel continued along the line, eventually stopping in front of Wing and Otto.

'You two also showed a glimmer of natural ability. With practice you might actually be only slightly embarrassing to watch.' Otto supposed that this might be as close as the Colonel got to a compliment. 'Unlike the rest of you maggots, whose collective performance fell somewhere between abysmal and outright terrible. By the time I'm finished I expect each of you Alphas to make that crossing in the blink of an eye and bone-dry. Do I make myself clear?' he growled.

'Sir, yes sir!' the students replied in unison.

The Colonel gave them an evil grin. 'I hope so, for

158

your sakes, because next time there might be something hungry in the water. Class dismissed.'

☻☻☻

'But if you move the quantum phase inverter it'll cause a catastrophic feedback loop.'

'Not if it's positioned before the induction array, it won't.'

Otto stared at the circuit diagram in front of him; the conversation with Laura was strangely exciting. He'd never met someone before who could argue so knowledgeably about complex technical issues, so it was refreshing to have this sort of discussion with someone who understood the ins and outs of advanced digital electronics. When Professor Pike had first announced that they would be partnered together for their Practical Technology lesson he had been worried that she would slow him down, but he was now realising that she was just as knowledgeable on the subject as he was, perhaps even more so. He was thoroughly enjoying their discussion of how the circuit diagram they had been given to study could be improved. Of course the test that they had been set had been only to spot the glaringly obvious errors in the design, but they had found all of those within the first two minutes.

The same could not be said for any of the other pairs of students seated at the workbenches around the room, who seemed to be struggling to understand the complex diagram that Professor Pike had handed out. He was certainly the least organised teacher that they had met so far; he had even arrived five minutes late. His scruffy unkempt appearance had changed little since Otto had first spotted him at the teachers' dining table. Otto suspected that he may even be wearing the exact same clothes that he had been the previous day. His stained white coat was worn over a battered tweed suit and his wild white hair looked as if it had never had more than a passing acquaintance with a brush. When he had hurried into the room he had been carrying a large pile of papers and books which he had unceremoniously dumped on to his desk, adding to the chaotic mess that was already present. He had not even introduced himself, but simply distributed the erroneous circuit diagrams before returning to his desk and studying the papers he had brought with him to the lesson.

Otto got the distinct impression that the students were a rather annoying distraction to the Professor, and that the exercise had been chosen because it would be time-consuming rather than particularly educational. At the very least it had given him a chance to talk properly to Laura. Wing, meanwhile, had been partnered with Nigel, and the pair of them seemed to be making little if any headway with the problem the Professor had presented to them. A couple of the students had complained that they really didn't understand the first thing about the diagram, but the Professor had told them that they should be more than capable of solving it and to try their best. To Otto, the diagram seemed to be part of a focusing system for an energy beam but, separated from its other components, it was impossible to tell what purpose it might serve beyond that.

'It could be part of one of those sleeper guns,' Laura mused, 'but the power output seems too high for that.'

Otto nodded. 'Whatever it is I reckon it'd be best not to be standing in front of it when it's activated.'

Laura smiled. 'Or possibly even on the same continent.'

Given some of the weapons that had been hinted at in their Villainy Studies lesson, this was probably no exaggeration.

'Fairly advanced stuff for our first day, though, wouldn't you say?' Laura continued, looking at the confused expressions on the faces of those around them.

'Maybe, but you don't seem to have much problem with it,' Otto observed.

'No, but this is what I'm best at – computers, electronics, that kind of thing. All the same, this design is highly advanced; it's a bit like giving someone Rachmaninoff to play at their first piano lesson, isn't it?'

Otto nodded. It was an unusually difficult challenge to be set in the first lesson, especially given that many of the other students in the class might never have had any experience with sophisticated electronics like this before. It was probably another one of H.I.V.E.'s tests, the technical equivalent of grappling over a chasm.

The Professor seemed hardly to notice that the class was taking place at all, continuing instead to study the documents he had brought with him to the lesson. The chaos on his desk was reflected in the rest of the classroom. It seemed as if every spare inch of space was taken up with bizarre unidentifiable devices or piles of paper. Behind the desk was a blackboard with 'DO NOT ERASE' written across the top in large block capitals. Beneath this firm instruction, filling every spare inch of the board, was an incredibly complex equation that Otto had lost track of after a couple of lines when it had delved into areas of mathematics with which he was unfamiliar. Clearly the Professor had a lot on his mind.

'So, did you get anything out of Shelby?' Otto asked Laura quietly.

Laura had sat chatting with Shelby at lunch, her impatience with her shower-hogging room-mate clearly forgotten after her display in the Tactical Education lesson that morning.

'No, she just said that she'd been a gymnast at school before she came here, and that it had seemed easy.' Laura's expression made it clear that she was less than satisfied with this explanation.

'Right, because normal gym lessons often include that kind of exercise, don't they?' Otto was as sceptical as Laura that this was a plausible explanation for Shelby's earlier performance.

'Well, I couldn't get anything else out of her. She just acted like it was perfectly normal and then changed the subject. I'll see if I can find out more this evening.' Laura looked over at Shelby, who was partnered with another girl on the other side of the room.

'Speaking of secrets, what did you do that caught H.I.V.E.'s attention?' Otto asked casually, still looking at the circuit diagram.

'Oh, I don't really know . . . er . . . is that a waveshift resistor?' Laura's clumsy attempt to change the subject could not hide the fact that her cheeks had suddenly turned red.

'No, it's a phase-alignment resistor.' Otto wasn't about to let her off the hook that easily. 'You must have some clue.'

'I could ask you the same question,' she replied softly.

'I asked you first.' Otto smiled at her and her cheeks went a slightly deeper shade of crimson.

'OK, but you have to promise not to tell anyone, and you have to tell me what landed you here as well,' she replied, giving him a serious look.

'It's a deal. So?'

'Well, it was nothing really. You see, there was this girl,

Mandy McTavish, at my old school, and I thought she was bitching about me behind my back but I didn't know what she was telling people. So I just listened in to a couple of her conversations on her mobile.' Laura looked slightly uncomfortable, and Otto knew that there had to be more to it than that.

'So H.I.V.E. recruited you because you eavesdropped on this girl? That's all?'

'Well, I didn't actually have the equipment I needed to listen in on her, so I had to borrow some.'

'Borrow?'

'Sort of. You see, there was an American air force base near our village and I used some of their equipment.'

'You broke into an air force base?' Otto couldn't keep the note of surprise from his voice.

'Not exactly. I just faked a security clearance and hacked into their computer network.' She looked even more embarrassed. 'They always had a couple of those AWACS early warning planes in the air and I just gave them some new surveillance orders for a few days, that's all.'

Otto grinned at her. 'Are you telling me that you used part of the nuclear attack early warning system to listen in on this girl gossiping about you?'

'I knew you'd think it was stupid,' she replied miserably. 'You promise not to tell anyone?'

'Of course.' Far from thinking she was stupid Otto was,

in fact, deeply impressed. The systems controlling the tasking of those planes would have had some of the most sophisticated anti-intrusion software in the world. It was easy to see why H.I.V.E. had taken such an interest in Laura. 'That's amazing, you shouldn't be embarrassed about it.'

She smiled sheepishly. 'I thought I'd covered my tracks, but obviously someone noticed what I was up to and I suppose that's how I ended up here.' Otto could tell from the way that she said it that she was as keen to get out of this place as he was. That could be useful – for the escape plan that was forming in his head to be successful he might need someone with Laura's talents.

'You sound like you'd like to get off this rock,' he whispered, 'I know how you feel.' He gave her a meaningful look.

'Do you have something in mind?' she asked quietly, pretending to study the diagram again.

'Perhaps. It's risky though.' Otto glanced up at the Professor but he was still studying the papers on his desk intently.

'No riskier than trying to survive in this place for the next few years,' she replied.

'OK, we'll talk later when it's a little more private.' There were too many ears in this room for him to say anything else. They might want to get off the island but that didn't mean that every student in the class felt the same way. They had to be cautious.

'OK,' Laura smiled at him. 'So what's your story, Otto? Come on, a deal's a deal.'

Otto hadn't really wanted to talk to anyone about this – he hadn't even discussed it with Wing – but he felt as if he could trust Laura not to tell anyone. Besides, she had the most striking green eyes he'd ever seen . . .

'Well, let's just say that the Prime Minister's funny turn a couple of days ago didn't come as any surprise to me . . .' He smiled as her eyes widened.

'That was you?' Laura's incredulous expression seemed to suggest that she found it hard to believe that Otto was the one responsible for the Prime Minister's involuntary resignation.

'Our secret, right?' Otto reminded her.

'Yeah, but how did you –'

'OK, time's up. Please bring your papers to my desk.' The Professor interrupted her question.

Otto picked up the diagram. 'I can be very persuasive when I want to be.' He was secretly delighted by the expression of shock on her face; he never normally got to share the details of his schemes with others. It was pointless to increase the chance of getting caught by boasting about his successes, but he knew that in this particular case it was a bit late to be worrying too much about that.

Otto walked up to the Professor's desk with their corrected circuit diagram. As he approached, the Professor looked up, a slightly confused expression on his face.

'Aren't you a little short for a final year student?' he asked, looking Otto up and down.

'Er . . . we're not final-year students, Professor, we're first years,' Otto replied, unsure as to what the Professor meant.

'But this is the advanced tech class. What are first years doing in my advanced tech class?' The Professor looked closely at the pips on Otto's collar. 'Oh dear.' He pulled a battered piece of paper from one of his lab coat pockets and examined it. 'Ah, yes, it would appear that my timetable is somewhat out of date. So you're first years, eh? I didn't think that I recognised many of you.' Clearly the chaotic mess in the lab was a reflection of its occupant's personality.

Otto handed the diagram to the Professor, aware that he and Laura probably shouldn't have been able to complete it. He certainly wished that they hadn't drawn the improved designs on the back.

'Yes, that exercise was probably a bit advanced for you. Sorry about that.' The Professor took the diagram and examined it closely. 'Still, you appear to have done rather well, Mr . . .?'

'Malpense, sir. Otto Malpense, and my partner Laura helped me a great deal with the exercise.'

'This really is quite excellent. I'd never considered using a variable phase array before, but it could work, yes.' The Professor appeared more interested in their suggested modifications to the design than enquiring about their ability to complete such an advanced challenge.

As the Professor studied the diagram Otto glanced down at the other papers strewn about his desk. He felt his heart jump as he realised what he was looking at. Those were blueprints of the school! He stared intently at the upside-down plans, committing them to memory in a fraction of a second. He closed his eyes briefly and could still see the blueprints in his mind's eye as clearly as if he had photographed them. This could be the break that they needed. He looked at some of the other papers on the desk. One in particular caught his attention, entitled 'Mk.2 Consciousness Transfer Device', but the details of the design were hidden under another sheet of paper.

Suddenly the Professor glanced back up at Otto, noticing him looking at the plans on his desk. He turned the blueprints over without saying anything and looked at Otto carefully.

'Well, this is rather a nuisance. I should have started with the basic tech course today, but by the looks of this diagram that might be a little bit simple for you two, wouldn't you say?' The Professor had the appearance of being scatterbrained, but Otto knew that it would be foolish to underestimate the man, all the same.

'Oh, I'm sure that we need to learn the basics too, Professor,' Otto replied carefully.

'Indeed you do, Otto, indeed you do.' The Professor's eyes narrowed slightly and Otto thought he saw a hint of a quite different side to the bumbling persona that the Professor projected. 'Let's see how the others have done, shall we?' Otto suddenly found himself wondering if it was an accident at all that they'd been given this advanced test. He wished that he and Laura had not completed the exercise so thoroughly; standing out from the crowd was probably not a good idea at H.I.V.E.

Other students were now approaching the desk with their papers, and it quickly became clear that Otto and Laura were the only pair who had made any progress with the test. The Professor was profuse in his apologies for the apparent misunderstanding and reassured the class that subsequent lessons would not be quite so challenging, much to the obvious relief of the class.

When Otto returned to their workbench Laura asked him how they had done with the exercise. He noticed that the Professor was watching them both closely.

'We did well,' he answered, 'perhaps a little too well.'

Chapter 10

It had been a long day for the new students and it was with some relief that they now headed to their final scheduled lesson, Stealth and Evasion. It had been quite unlike any school day that they had experienced before and Otto found himself wondering if every day would be as unconventional as this or if they'd just been given an educational baptism of fire.

The students filed through the doors into a lecture theatre with rows of banked seating. There was no sign of the teacher, Ms Leon, but Otto did at least now know who the pampered cat that he had seen at lunch the previous day belonged to. The fluffy white cat lay curled on the desk at the front of the room, apparently sleeping, oblivious to the presence of the Alpha students.

After a minute or two all of the class had sat down and were talking amongst themselves, waiting for the teacher to arrive. The noise had obviously disturbed the cat, who stood up and stretched on the front desk, fixing the assembled children with an inquisitive look.

'Good afternoon, children.' The woman's voice had a French accent and seemed to be coming from the front of the room, but there was still no sign of the teacher. Everyone fell silent, curious as to where this disembodied voice was coming from.

'My name is Ms Leon. Welcome to your first Stealth and Evasion lesson.'

Otto and Wing looked at each other in amazement. *The voice was coming from the cat!*

'You will have to excuse my present condition. Suffice to say that Professor Pike's initial experiments imbuing humans with the abilities of certain animals have not been as successful as he might have liked. I believe that he would describe it as semi-permanent consciousness transfer, but the simpler explanation is that, thanks to technology that was rather more experimental than I was led to believe, I am now resident in this body while my rather confused cat is enjoying the use of opposable thumbs for the first time.'

Over the past two days Otto had seen any number of strange things, but this was on an altogether different plane of strangeness. Mouths were hanging open in shock all around the room.

'Judging by your expressions you find this a little

171

unusual, but let me assure you that your shock is fairly minor in comparison to waking up for the first time with a tail. That sort of thing can ruin your whole day. The good Professor assures me that he will, in time, be able to reverse the process, but for the moment you will all have to get used to my current form. Which, strangely, does have its advantages.' With that, the cat sprang two metres from the desk at the front of the room and landed flawlessly on a tall stool that was positioned in front of the students.

'The purpose of this class is quite simple: to teach you how to remain unseen by those who would seek you out, how to move and act silently – a discipline that will doubtless be of use to you in the years to come. By the time this course is complete you should be able to move unnoticed through even the most highly secured envir-onments.'

Judging by the expressions on most of the students' faces, they were still trying to accept the fact that a cat was talking to them, rather than wondering exactly what these lessons would teach them. Otto had noticed that when Ms Leon had been addressing the class the cat's mouth had not been moving, and he was curious to know how exactly she was managing to speak to them at all. He looked at the sparkling jewelled collar that the cat was wearing and saw that what he had originally taken to be a bright blue jewel at her throat was actually a blue LED. He guessed that it must actually be some kind of speech synthesis unit, and that H.I.V.E.mind was probably playing a significant part in providing her with a voice.

Otto heard a boy seated behind him whisper to his neighbour, 'Do you think she's got a litter tray or a toilet?'

Ms Leon moved so quickly that she appeared to be little more than a white blur, leaping past the students. Otto turned in his seat to see the cat sitting on the desk behind him, a single razor-sharp claw hooked into the nostril of the boy who had made the comment, his face a mask of sudden terror.

'A cat can hear a mouse moving through grass thirty metres away on a windy day, so you might as well have shouted that little witticism to the whole room, you stupid little boy. Just so you know, the claw that is very nearly breaking your skin right now is only one of eighteen. All just as sharp as that one and I know exactly where all the softest, most vulnerable parts of your body are. Bearing that in mind, do you have any other jokes that you would like to share with the class?'

'No, Ms Leon,' the boy replied in a shaky voice. His face had gone quite pale.

'Good.' She retracted the claw, releasing the terrified boy, and leapt from desk to desk back to the front of the room.

'We will start with some of the basics of surveillance avoidance to better prepare you for your first practical exercises.' Otto noticed now that the LED flickered slightly as she spoke – it appeared that his suspicions were correct.

For the next twenty minutes Ms Leon sat on the stool and talked to them about the basic principles of infiltration and counter-surveillance. Otto was surprised at how quickly he and his fellow students adjusted to the fact that they were being taught by an animal, but he supposed that, like him, the other students were becoming somewhat immunised to such bizarre situations by their experiences at H.I.V.E. so far.

'So, it is important that you learn to recognise the patterns inherent in a surveillance system, to spot the gaps and exploit them . . . I'm sorry, Miss Trinity. Am I boring you?'

Otto glanced over at Shelby just in time to see her stop doodling on her notepad and quickly sit up straighter in her seat, a slightly embarrassed expression on her face.

'Perhaps you think that there is nothing that I can teach you, hmm?' Ms Leon continued. 'What with all the practical experience you have had of this.'

Laura, who was sitting next to Shelby, gave her roommate a curious look.

Ms Leon tilted her head, her whiskers twitched. 'Oh,

don't tell me that you haven't told anyone yet. You should know that we don't have to keep secrets at H.I.V.E. We're all friends here Shelby, or would you prefer me to call you the Wraith?'

It was as if the mask had slipped from Shelby's face for the first time. Her expression hardened and she fixed the white cat with a cold stare.

'I don't know what you're talking about,' Shelby replied evenly, never breaking eye contact with Ms Leon.

'No, of course you don't. I suppose that you must have qualified for the Alpha stream because of your immaculate manicure. It couldn't possibly have anything to do with the fact that you might know something about the several million dollars' worth of jewellery that have mysteriously disappeared from some of the world's most secure locations over the past twelve months. That would be ridiculous, would it not?' The expression on Shelby's face suggested that she knew exactly what Ms Leon was talking about. Students all around the room were nudging each other and whispering. The Wraith had become something of a celebrity over the past few months, a thief who seemed to pass straight through supposedly impregnable security systems, leaving no trace of their passing and stealing only the very finest, most exquisite pieces of jewellery. The only mark that the thief had left at each location was a card inscribed 'My thanks, the Wraith', resting where a spectacularly valuable piece of jewellery had once sat. At first the insurance companies and security firms had managed to keep this quiet, but eventually the press had got hold of the information. The story had stimulated the public imagination and there had been much speculation as to who this apparently invisible thief might be. Otto suspected that very few people would have believed that these robberies were actually the work of a thirteen-year-old girl. Shelby looked more angry than embarrassed that not only did Ms Leon appear to know exactly who she was but had chosen to announce this fact to the entire class.

'I don't suppose that there's much point trying to deny it, is there?' Shelby's voice had a cold, hard edge that Otto had not heard before. The grating Valley girl persona that she had displayed up till now had vanished.

'Hardly, *chéri*. I have been following your exploits with some interest. You show . . . promise. A diamond in the rough, so to speak. You have a rare natural talent – it is not something you need to be coy about or hide from people here.' Ms Leon finally broke eye contact with Shelby and addressed the whole class again. 'Anyway, as I was saying, recognition of surveillance patterns is vital if . . .'

As Ms Leon continued with the class, Shelby seemed to be listening more attentively than before, seemingly oblivious to the fact that she had suddenly become the centre of the other students' attention. Otto knew he couldn't be the only one who noted the way she was glaring at their new teacher. This might be an interesting battle of wills, he thought to himself.

The class finally ended, bringing their first day of lessons to a close, and Ms Leon, having dismissed them, trotted out of the classroom with her tail waving in the air. Several of the students approached Shelby, clearly intrigued to meet the celebrity who had been hiding in their midst, but the withering look that she gave them as they approached obviously made them think better of it and they hastily retreated. Laura, however, was not so easily deterred.

'So were you planning to tell me about this at any point?' she asked as Shelby packed her books into her backpack.

'Not if I could help it, but it looks like anonymity isn't something that people have a whole lot of respect for around here,' Shelby replied, angrily shoving the last of her books into her bag.

'You could have told me. I wouldn't have told anyone, you know.'

'Look, it's not something that I wanted to talk about. I just wanted to get off this damn island as quickly as possible and go back to my old life, but now everyone knows who I am, how am I supposed to do that?' Shelby replied angrily. 'Just leave me alone, will you?'

Laura took a step back, hand raised. 'OK, OK. I just wanted to see if you were all right, that's all.'

'I'm fine,' Shelby snapped, and pushed past Laura, heading for the door.

Otto and Wing walked over to Laura, who had a look of concern on her face as she watched Shelby leave.

'Is she OK?' Otto asked.

'Not really. I think she hoped she was going to keep that secret a wee bit longer.'

'It does seem unfair that she should be exposed so publicly,' Wing added, 'but she would not have been able to keep her true identity hidden for long. Consider her performance with the grappler earlier. You may be able to hide your identity, but it is much harder to hide your abilities.'

Otto thought about this. They had all indeed shown hints of exceptional ability throughout the day and it did feel as if they had each been somehow tricked into displaying what they were truly capable of. He knew he might just be being paranoid, but it did seem to him that they were teaching the staff as much about their own capabilities as they themselves were being taught. He didn't know what Dr Nero might do with such information, but he had little doubt that the staff would dutifully report the various events of the day back to him.

'Now I am seeing everything. A talking cat, what next?' Franz asked as he joined them.

'Well, Block and Tackle are talking apes, so I suppose it's not that surprising really,' Otto replied with a grin. 'Although it does suggest that volunteering for Professor Pike's experiments may not be a very good idea.'

'Oh, it can't be all that bad.' Laura smiled. 'Don't cats sleep for seventy-five per cent of the day? I certainly feel like I could handle that at the moment.'

Otto knew what she meant. He was exhausted and his shoulders ached from swinging around in the grappler cavern earlier. His brain, too, felt overloaded with information, trying to analyse all they'd seen and heard. Whatever more sinister reason there might be for confronting them with so many strange situations throughout the day, it had certainly guaranteed that they were kept off-balance.

Nigel wandered over and started chatting to Franz about the events of the day, giving Laura an opportunity to pull Otto and Wing to one side. Looking around to check that nobody was listening in on them, she whispered, 'Shelby wants out of here too. Do you think it's worth talking to her about what we discussed earlier?'

Wing raised an eyebrow at Otto. Clearly he was a little

179

surprised that their informal escape committee had been extended to include her as a member.

'Maybe. Why don't you try to talk to her later, when she's cooled down a bit,' Otto suggested.

'We should be cautious. We do not yet really know who we can trust,' Wing added. The brief look that he gave Otto implied that he was not sure that they should even be discussing this yet with Laura.

'I know, but we can't do this alone. We're going to need all the help we can get, and her experience at getting past security systems unobserved could be useful. Speak to her, but try to make it as casual as possible. There's a lot we don't really know about her yet,' Otto reminded Laura.

'That's true of all of us, Otto. We have to trust each other if we're really going to get out of here,' Laura replied.

Otto nodded. 'I know, but just be careful. If the staff gets any hint of what we're up to, we could be leaving the island in boxes.'

☢☢☢

An invitation to dinner from Dr Nero was not something that any member of the teaching staff at H.I.V.E. was given the option of refusing. And so it was that the Contessa, Professor Pike and Colonel Francisco were now seated at Dr Nero's dining-room table talking amongst themselves, awaiting the arrival of their host. Ms Leon was also there, sitting upon a large red velvet cushion on top of a chair that raised her to the level of the table. The room would not have looked out of place in an English country home, and only the lack of windows served as a reminder that they were deep underground. A member of Nero's personal staff busied himself around the room, bringing in serving dishes and pouring drinks for the Doctor's guests. After a couple of minutes Nero finally entered the room.

'I'm sorry to have kept you waiting. There were matters that I had to attend to that detained me longer than I anticipated.' He turned to the white-coated attendant. 'Ivan, please serve the first course.'

Ivan dutifully began to ladle soup into bowls and served them to the assembled diners, with the exception of Ms Leon who was served finely chopped smoked salmon in a silver bowl.

'So, how did our new Alphas cope with their first day? I trust that there were no unforeseen difficulties?' Nero asked his guests.

'Their performance was as anticipated,' Francisco replied. 'You were right about the girl, she showed remarkable proficiency. The others performed as expected – Fanchu and Malpense proved capable, but the rest of the class were typically lacking. It'll take some time but I'll get them all up to scratch eventually.'

Nero nodded. 'Tabitha, any problems?'

Ms Leon looked up from her bowl. 'No. As you expected, Miss Trinity had not revealed her true identity to her classmates but now, if you'll excuse the obvious pun, the cat is well and truly out of the bag. I suspect that she is feeling suitably exposed.'

'Good. It may have been that she would have shared the true details of her past with her companions in time, but I'd rather not delay things any longer than necessary.' Nero turned to Professor Pike. 'Professor, did your lesson proceed as planned?'

'Yes, Malpense performed as predicted, but the Brand girl was more capable than I had expected. It appears that her fundamental understanding of technology is not just limited to computers. I might even use a couple of the alterations that they suggested in the new version of the Poseidon device – power consumption efficiency could be improved by as much as twenty-five per cent. Their innovative use of distributed phase arrays could create a geometrically scaled multiplication in damping resonance by –'

'Thank you, Professor, perhaps we can go over the finer details later. Did everything else go smoothly?' Nero asked.

'Malpense behaved just as you predicted, Doctor.'

'Excellent.' Nero had not shared the details of Malpense's sponsor with the rest of those around the table – he had too many unanswered questions of his own to announce Number One's personal interest in the boy just yet. Thankfully the staff were used to Nero focusing on one or two pupils from every new intake, so they would not consider his interest in the boy to be anything particularly unusual. Ever since Nero had singled Diabolus Darkdoom out for special attention all those years ago the staff had exhibited remarkable faith in his ability to spot potential in this way.

'If those two are such technical geniuses, perhaps you could enlist their help in trying to return me to my proper shape, Professor. It would seem that you require some assistance.' Ms Leon made no attempt to hide the note of contempt in her voice.

'I have told you I'm working on it. This was an unanticipated side effect. It will take time to reverse safely. If you would just submit to a few more tests, I could –'

'You'll understand, I'm sure, Professor, if I am somewhat reluctant to submit myself to any more of your experimental procedures. Your success rate has been rather disappointing of late. While there is undoubtedly some novelty value to this body I do grow tired of hearing your excuses for your apparent inability to correct your mistakes.' The fur along Ms Leon's back bristled slightly as she spoke.

'I warned you the procedure was experimental, but you insisted –'

'You told me that it might not work, you did not tell me that there was a chance I would wake up with an irresistible temptation to chase balls of wool around the floor of my quarters. I was promised agility and heightened senses, not hairballs and claws. Perhaps I should find new ways to motivate your efforts.' Ms Leon raised one of her paws in the air, flexing her razor-sharp claws from their sheaths.

'Don't threaten me, Tabitha, or perhaps you'd rather stay as you are –'

'Enough!' Nero looked angry. 'I am tired of listening to you arguing about this. Number One personally instructed the Professor to continue this research, and I can think of no better motivation than the thought of disappointing *him*. Tabitha, I understand your frustration but you must be patient. Your original body is quite safe in the cryogenic chamber, and as soon as the procedure can be reversed it will be. And you, Professor, should redouble your efforts. Number One expects results, not excuses, and you know quite well that he is not a man renowned for his patience.'

The two teachers fell silent. They had learnt long ago not to push their luck with Nero. He was concerned, though, that these clashes were becoming more frequent, and he wondered how much longer he would be able to keep them from each other's throats. Quite literally, in Ms Leon's case.

'What about Darkdoom's son?' the Contessa asked. 'Surely he is worth watching too?'

'I'm not sure,' Nero replied. 'I had hoped that confronting him with a history of his father's achievements would help motivate him, but he does not strike me as being quite the boy that his father was when he arrived here.'

'He may just need time to adjust,' the Contessa replied. 'I would hate to think that my efforts in *persuading* his mother to let him attend the school were wasted.'

'I take it that he is not aware of the true circumstances of his father's death yet?' the Colonel asked, taking a swig from his glass. The question made the other teachers look uncomfortable.

'No,' Nero replied, 'and I expect you all to ensure that it stays that way. We have quite enough to worry about at the moment as it is.'

Chapter 11

For Otto and the other students their timetable remained unforgiving over the next couple of months; their new education proceeded at a breakneck pace that showed no sign of letting up any time soon. One moment they would be learning how to crack the latest design of high-security vault, the next they would be studying the logistics of building secret orbital launch facilities. The work was relentless, and there seemed to be little room at H.I.V.E. for those who could not maintain this punishing pace. Otto was finding the work challenging but not impossible, his own strange talents helping him to adapt quickly to this new way of life. The only problems he had were with the Politics and Economics classes, not because they were particularly difficult, but because he found them mind-numbingly dull. Like anyone else he found it hard to excel in subjects that he had little or no interest in. Franz, on the other hand, had displayed a remarkable natural talent for 'creative' accountancy – it seemed that he could hide or redistribute money in such a way that even the teachers could not trace what he had done with the fictional funds in their exercises.

Wing too had continued to excel in Tactical Education. Indeed, something of a friendly rivalry had developed between him and Shelby over the course of a few more of the Colonel's lessons, and their races across the grappler cavern were quickly becoming more and more hair-raising to watch. Shelby had proven to be a quite different person after she had been unmasked so publicly in their first lesson with Ms Leon. Gone was the spoilt brat persona that she had adopted in the first couple of days, replaced instead with a quiet confidence and occasional displays of hilarious but withering sarcasm. Shelby had not forgiven Ms Leon for her announcement of her true identity to the class, and as Otto had watched them verbally sparring over the following weeks he was reminded of two prize fighters circling each other, looking for the opening that would allow one of them to deliver the knockout blow. Otto doubted that Shelby would have been allowed to get away with this if it weren't for the fact that she performed so brilliantly in the Stealth and Evasion classes. Her professional name had been well earned, since it seemed that she could be as invisible as a ghost when she wanted to be.

Shelby and Laura had also become fast friends, partly due to long late-night conversations in their room and partly due to the fact that Laura had succeeded in persuading Shelby to join their scheme to get off the island. Initially she had been reluctant to join them, insisting that she 'worked better alone' but soon she realised, just as Otto had, that escaping would take their combined efforts if it was going to be possible at all.

In fact the only person who seemed to be really struggling to adapt to life at H.I.V.E. was Nigel. For several days it had seemed that each new lesson they attended just made him more miserable, not helped by the fact that all of the teachers seemed to have higher expectations of him than they had of the other students. Otto had lost count of the number of times that he had been picked on by a teacher, singled out to answer a particularly difficult question or had his poor performance compared unfavourably with the past successes of his father. Clearly the Darkdoom name was a burden that he was expected to bear without complaint, but Otto had grave doubts that Nigel was really a suitable candidate for the Alpha stream. The only subject with which he didn't seem to struggle was Biotechnology, often displaying a depth of knowledge of the subject that had surprised the teachers and even his fellow students. Consequently, the only place where Nigel seemed happy was in the hydroponics lab, where he had quickly become fascinated with the carnivorous plants that H.I.V.E. cultivated for experimental purposes. Otto had accepted an invitation from Nigel to come and feed his charges with him one evening after dinner and he had been struck by the care with which Nigel had fed insects to each of the numerous varieties of plants.

'I used to tend the gardens with my mother,' he had explained, 'this reminds me of home.'

Homesickness was not something that Otto found he suffered from, but in that regard he seemed to be the exception rather than the rule. Laura had been missing her parents particularly badly, refusing to believe that they could possibly have consented to her abduction. She wanted to get home, believing that they would be worried sick by her disappearance and frustrated that she could not reassure them that she was OK. This was just one reason why their 'extra-curricular' activities had been proceeding quickly. If they were going to escape, they needed to act fast. The longer they spent on the island, the greater the chance that their efforts would be discovered.

It had not been until the end of their first month at H.I.V.E. that Otto had explained the details of his plan to Wing, Laura and Shelby. The four of them had sat in a quiet corner of the atrium as Otto had explained to them exactly how they were going to escape, his voice low to avoid any chance of being overheard. As Otto had predicted, they had initially greeted his suggestion with open scepticism. Shelby in particular seemed highly dubious that the four of them were capable of doing what Otto was suggesting while still avoiding detection. Otto had been prepared for this and had reassured his three co-conspirators by going through each stage of the plan in detail and providing apparently satisfactory answers to all of their many questions. After a couple of these secretive meetings it seemed that they were all starting to really believe that they could actually pull it off, and Otto turned their attention to solving some of the initial practical problems that had to be overcome before any escape attempt could be mounted.

First he had gone over the list of components that he and Laura would require in order to construct some of the equipment they'd need. Otto thought that he could smuggle some of the more common items out of Practical Technology lessons himself. Professor Pike was not, after all, renowned for keeping a particularly close eye on the students during his lessons. Some of the more *exotic* components, however, would be rather more difficult for them to lay their hands on. He knew where some of them could be acquired, but the security around them might be tight. He had discussed these items with Shelby and she had, after a couple of days of discreet investigation, assured him that she could get them what they needed without being detected. It was Otto's turn to be sceptical then – he knew that she was uniquely gifted when it came to acquiring hard-to-reach items, but this would be a real test of her prowess.

It was no small surprise, then, when after only a couple of days Shelby had walked into Otto and Wing's quarters and carefully laid out on the bed every single item on the list. Otto made a mental note that he would remember in future to have more faith in her abilities. That had been the cue for Otto and Laura to start work on assembling these components into something they could use. Otto was ninety-nine per cent certain, after searching every inch of their rooms, that there was no surveillance of the students in their quarters, and so they had decided to use their bathrooms as makeshift workshops for this purpose. The way he saw it, if they were being watched as they worked on these unapproved science projects then they would doubtless find out soon enough. The fact that they had eventually completed their work without the ever-present guards breaking down their bathroom doors suggested that their activities had thankfully remained undetected.

And so it was, as they approached the end of November, that they were finally ready to put their plan into action. There were still elements of the scheme that worried Otto, places where they might have to rely rather too much on luck for his liking, but they could not afford to sit around worrying. They finally settled on a date for their attempt and, as the fateful day drew nearer, Otto could not help but feel nervous and a little excited. There was no doubt that H.I.V.E. was a unique establishment, and much of what they'd studied he'd found fascinating, but he still felt like a laboratory rat in a maze. Secretly he feared that if he stayed much longer he might start to enjoy his studies rather too much, which would only make it that much harder to leave. There was a nagging voice at the back of his mind that kept asking what exactly it was that he was so keen to get back to. The orphanage may have been his home for years, but he didn't miss it as much as he thought he would, and it wasn't as if he could spend the rest of his life there. The louder this voice got the more determined Otto became that he had to leave now before these doubts became impossible to ignore.

☢ ☢ ☢

'So, with such a potent combination of natural neuro-toxins it is easy to see why this particular family of plants has so much potential. Full-scale cultivation may even –'
    MWAH, MWAAAAH, MWAH!!!!

The school bell echoed around the hydroponics dome, drowning out the final words of Ms Gonzales's Biotechnology lesson. As everyone started to pack their bags she raised her voice.

'Remember I want you all to complete an essay on the genetic manipulation of growth characteristics in complex plants for next week's lesson.'

Otto couldn't help but smile to himself. If all went to plan tonight he wouldn't have to worry about that particular piece of homework. Wing caught sight of Otto's expression and grinned.

'Perhaps we should post our essays to her,' he said quietly.

'We could if we had an address to send them to,' Otto replied, and, noticing Nigel approaching, quickly placed a finger to his lips, silencing Wing.

'Hi guys.' Nigel seemed unusually cheerful. 'Are you going straight to lunch or have you got a couple of minutes to have a look at something I've been working on?'

Otto swung his backpack on to his shoulder. 'I'm in no hurry to get to lunch. Let's see what the mysterious Darkdoom has been up to his in lab.'

Nigel smiled happily at Otto. 'Cool. Do you want to come too, Wing?'

'Certainly, though I don't mind telling you that I find

those insect-eating plants of yours rather unsettling.' Wing wasn't joking. He didn't like the way that an apparently innocent-looking plant could hide the fact that it was a killer, even if it did only murder bugs.

'Oh, this is much better than them, trust me,' Nigel replied, sounding strangely proud. 'Come on.' He beckoned for Otto and Wing to follow him up a nearby flight of stairs.

They passed through an airtight door and down a long gantry that hung above the steaming tropical environment that was artificially maintained in this part of the dome. Eventually they came to a door which Nigel opened to reveal a small room with glass walls that looked out on the carefully cultivated jungle below. In the centre of the one workbench in the tiny room was a large cube-shaped object covered with a black cloth.

'Please speak quietly – she's very sensitive to sound,' Nigel whispered.

Wing glanced at Otto as Nigel turned to the cloth-covered object, a look of confused curiosity on his face. Otto gave a small shrug in reply. It had been a couple of weeks since Nigel had excitedly announced that Ms Gonzales was letting him use one of the spare rooms in the hydroponics dome to conduct extra research. Otto remembered feeling pleased that Nigel had found something to interest him at H.I.V.E., especially given his dismal performance in their other classes. Now it seemed that they were finally going to get to see what he'd been doing in this tiny little room.

'Here, come closer,' Nigel instructed, and Otto and Wing obediently crowded round the mysterious cube.

'Gentlemen, it is my great pleasure to introduce you to Violet.' Nigel pulled the cover from the cube with a flourish to reveal a glass tank containing the strangest plant that either of them had ever seen. It looked like a single Venus flytrap at the end of a fifteen-centimetre-long stem, but it had long sharp thorns in its mouth rather than the soft flexible fronds that made up the normal plant's 'teeth'. Arranged around the base of the stem were prickly leaves and long tendrils that occasionally waved around in the air, as if seeking prey. Nigel seemed delighted by the amazed looks on Otto and Wing's faces.

'Isn't she beautiful?' Nigel sighed. 'It's taken me ages to sequence the right characteristics from my other plants, but she's been worth all the work.' He popped open a plastic box on the workbench and pulled out a long fat earthworm. 'Watch this.'

Nigel dropped the earthworm on the soil near the base of the plant; Violet's reaction was swift and violent. The tendrils at the plant's base snaked out, gripping the worm as the toothed jaw bent down on its flexible stem with

195

startling speed, snatching up the helpless creature, devouring it in seconds. Wing's expression turned to fascinated revulsion.

'That is truly one of the most disturbing things I have ever seen,' he said softly. 'How did you create this thing?'

'Oh, just a slightly modified gene here, a bit of judicious cross-pollination there. You know, the usual.' Nigel looked as if he was going to burst with pride.

'She's amazing, Nigel, just amazing,' Otto said, unable to tear his eyes away from the final moments of the unfortunate worm's existence.

'I haven't shown her to Ms Gonzales yet. I'm worried that they might *experiment* on her. So you mustn't tell anyone, OK?' He fixed them with a serious look – this was clearly very important to him.

'My lips are sealed, Nigel, don't worry.' Otto reminded himself that after this evening he wouldn't be able to tell anyone else at H.I.V.E. about Violet, even if he wanted to.

'You can count on my discretion,' Wing said seriously, 'as long as you promise never to feed her in front of me again.'

'Thanks, guys,' Nigel smiled again, 'I really appreciate it. You know how badly I'm doing in my other classes. I don't want to mess up Biotech as well. I just wish I could show her to my mum, she'd be so proud.'

Otto felt a familiar twinge of guilt. On more than one occasion he and Wing had sat discussing late into the night whether or not they should take Nigel with them when they left. Unfortunately they just kept coming to the same conclusion – Nigel was a liability. There was no way that he'd be able to keep up with them when they made their break for it – he would just slow them down in a situation where speed would be everything. It didn't stop Otto from feeling terrible that they were going to be leaving the small bald boy behind.

'She's only two days old. You should see the rate she's been growing, and she hasn't stopped yet. In a few weeks' time you won't recognise her.' Nigel looked proudly at the plant, which seemed to have gone quite still. 'She always rests after a kill,' he explained. 'Doesn't she look cute?'

Otto thought that this was probably his and Wing's cue to leave.

'Come on, Wing. Watching Violet eat has made me hungry. We'd better go and get some lunch before it's all gone.'

Wing nodded. 'Are you coming, Nigel?'

'No, I want to run a couple more tests on Violet. I'll see you guys later. Thanks for coming up and meeting her.' Nigel replied happily.

'Any time, Nigel. We'll have to come up and see her

again in a few days,' Otto replied. He was still feeling guilty about having to lie to Nigel as they left him talking happily to his new friend.

☺☺☺

Otto, Wing, Shelby and Laura sat at a table in one of the more secluded corners of the dining hall, talking quietly amongst themselves as they ate.

'Everything's set, then. We go tonight,' Otto whispered, looking around carefully to ensure that there weren't any potential eavesdroppers within hearing range.

'Ready as we'll ever be,' Laura replied. 'I still wish there was some way that we could test the primary device before we go, but we'll just have to pray that me and Otto got our sums right.'

'Try not to overfill me with confidence, won't you?' Shelby replied sarcastically, looking uncharacteristically nervous.

'We know it will work, the theory's sound,' Otto reassured her. 'The parts you got were perfect, there's no reason it shouldn't go smoothly.' He tried to sound more confident than he felt. He too wished there was a way they could conduct more tests, but the very nature of the device meant that it was going to be a one-shot deal.

'If we stick to the plan, we will be successful,' Wing said calmly. He seemed to be immune to the nervousness that the others were feeling. 'We must simply hope that we do not encounter any unforeseen circumstances.'

Wing was right. Otto knew that there were risks they couldn't completely eliminate, but he too was more worried about the wildcard factors that could completely derail the plan than anything else.

'Just keep your eyes open over the next few hours for anything that might cause any problems. Once we start this we can't stop – it's all or nothing.' Otto knew that the tiniest detail might be important.

'Do or die, huh?' Shelby replied.

Otto smiled grimly. 'Yes, if not the precise words I would have chosen.'

☻☻☻

Otto and Wing left Shelby and Laura in the dining hall. It was best that they kept apart from each other now; they all knew what they had to do. Wing appeared distracted as they walked towards the accommodation block. He was unusually quiet.

'Something on your mind?' Otto asked.

'There is one thing I am not sure about. If the plan is successful and we make it back to civilisation, do we tell people about H.I.V.E.?' Wing asked. It was a question that Otto had already given considerable thought to.

'No, we don't,' Otto replied firmly.

'Why not? What about the other students here?' Wing didn't seem happy with Otto's opinion.

'For the same reason that once you've sneaked past a wasp's nest in a tree you don't return and start hitting it with a stick,' Otto replied.

'I'm not sure what you mean.' Wing stopped walking and turned to face Otto. 'Surely it is our duty to try to free the others. We can't just walk away.'

'That's exactly what we're going to do. If we expose the school, they're going to know exactly who was responsible, and I guarantee you that they will not rest until all four of us are dealt with . . . permanently.' Otto doubted that Wing had given this as much thought as he had.

'So we should be silenced by fear?'

Otto tried to keep his voice calm. Wing could be infuriating to argue with about things like this – he seemed to see everything in black and white. 'No, we should disappear. H.I.V.E. can't kill what it can't find. Besides which, what do you think would happen to the other students if H.I.V.E. was exposed? Do you really think that Nero's going to thank them for their time and wave them on their way? No, they'll cover it up, and if that means covering up the students too, that's exactly what they'll do . . . with concrete, probably.'

Wing looked carefully at Otto, as if trying to see what he was thinking.

'I suppose you're right,' Wing sighed. 'It still seems unfair to just abandon the others to their fate like that, though.'

'A worse fate would await them if we spilled the beans about this place.' Otto stopped suddenly, spotting someone approaching down the corridor. 'Oh no . . .' Wing turned round to see Block and Tackle standing just ten metres away; Block was holding a length of steel pipe.

'Oh dear, looks like we found a couple of maggots who lost their way, Mr Tackle,' Block said, tapping the pipe into his palm.

'We should show them where to go, Mr Block,' Tackle replied, grinning. Otto suddenly noticed how very deserted the corridor seemed as the two thugs advanced towards them.

'Get behind me,' Wing instructed Otto. 'When they attack, run.'

'No way, Wing. I'm not leaving you alone with those two.' Otto sounded braver than he felt. He doubted very much that he had any chance of disabling either of the two hulking henchmen in the same way that he had done in the dining hall on their first day. A nerve pinch might be an effective way of dealing with someone once, but its success depended very much on the element of surprise, which was something he no longer had. Unfortunately the steel pipe that Block was wielding suggested that this time Block and Tackle were playing for keeps.

'Very well, leave the one with the pipe to me. Hold the other one off for as long as possible. If I go down, promise me you'll run,' Wing replied, not taking his eyes off their two assailants for a second.

'If you go down, I'm sure it will be after me.' Otto swallowed hard, suddenly frightened. Fear was something he didn't feel often, and he hated it – it made him feel weak and confused.

Wing took a single step towards the two brutes, stopping them short. He had adopted a fighting stance, and doubt briefly flickered across the two henchmen's faces.

Wing spoke, his voice calm and clear. 'There are twenty-three ways of combatting an assailant armed with a blunt object from this position. Four of them will kill you, twelve of them will permanently disable you and the remaining seven will cause injuries that, while being extremely painful, you will at least recover from. In all of them I take that pipe from you and use it on you. The choice is yours.'

Suddenly the looks of smug confidence vanished from Block and Tackle's faces. Block looked nervously at his companion, his voice uncertain.

'Come on, let's get out of here.' He turned away from

Wing, as if to retreat back up the corridor. Then, with a murderous roar, he spun back towards Wing, swinging the pipe in a vicious arc straight at his head.

Wing moved blindingly fast, his hand snapping up and catching the pipe with a loud slapping noise, catching Block off balance. He stepped in towards the hulking boy and twisted the pipe neatly from his hand, spinning it in his own hand and planting a swift blow to his attacker's stomach. Block doubled up, clutching his belly, all of the wind knocked from him. Seeing this, Tackle let out a roar and swung a clenched fist the size of a melon straight at Wing's face. Wing deflected the blow upwards, throwing Tackle off balance, and planted a vicious jab with his other hand right into Tackle's armpit, causing the larger boy to bellow in pain. The two assailants backed off a couple of yards as Wing threw the pipe away over his shoulder and returned calmly to the same stance he had adopted bare seconds before. Tackle's arm hung limp at his side, apparently disabled by Wing's punch, and Block stood gasping, still trying to catch his breath.

'Think . . . you're pretty . . . tough, do ya?' Block managed to gasp out between strained breaths, glaring malevolently at Wing.

'No, but I think you are clumsy and slow,' Wing replied, his voice calm. It was an observation more than a taunt.

'You'll be clumsy too when I've broken all your fingers,' Tackle growled, circling round to Wing's left. Block moved in the opposite direction, apparently attempting to surround Wing. Otto quietly picked the pipe up from the floor nearby where Wing had discarded it. Suddenly, both the henchman students charged Wing at once. Wing sprang into the air, his foot catching the stampeding Block neatly under the chin, snapping the thug's head back and sending him collapsing backwards on to the floor. Tackle made a grab for Wing as his companion collapsed, but Wing ducked and planted a jab identical to the first – this time, though, into Tackle's other armpit. Again the larger boy howled in pain, backing away rapidly. Wing advanced on Tackle, who seemed to still be struggling to get his arms to respond to basic commands.

'Stop this, I do not want to hurt you more seriously,' Wing said calmly as he walked towards the retreating Tackle.

'Yeah? Well, I *do* want to hurt you more seriously,' Tackle replied and reached into his overalls, pulling out a vicious-looking knife.

'Wing! Catch!' Otto shouted and threw the pipe to his friend. It spun end over end through the air and Wing turned at the last moment to catch it . . . with his forehead. He grunted and fell to the floor, out cold. Otto's eyes widened in horror. What had he done?

The momentary look of surprise on Tackle's face was replaced with an evil grin. He looked down at the unconscious form of Wing.

'I'll be back for you in a second, karate kid,' he looked up at Otto, 'but you're first, Whitey.'

Otto looked desperately around the hallway for something to defend himself with as Tackle approached. Block too had risen to his feet and picked up the pipe that lay next to Wing, joining Tackle as they advanced down the corridor towards Otto.

'Gonna leave you a greasy spot on the floor, Maggot,' Block growled as he approached. Otto had nowhere to run.

Well, I'm going to go out fighting, Otto thought to himself, adopting the same fighting stance that Wing had used a few seconds earlier. He hoped desperately that Tackle and Block might not realise that he didn't have the first clue how to defend himself in the same way Wing had.

Suddenly Block and Tackle's eyes widened in terror. Block dropped the pipe to the floor with a clatter and backed away, hand raised defensively before him.

'I'm sorry, I'm sorry! Please don't hurt me, oh God!' Block squealed pathetically. He turned and fled back up the corridor.

'We were only messing around, we weren't really

gonna hurt anyone,' Tackle squeaked, dropping the knife and racing down the corridor in pursuit of his friend. Otto was astonished. Had he really presented that fierce a challenge?

What Otto had not seen as the two henchmen approached him was the black-clad figure that unfolded itself from the shadows in the roof of the corridor and dropped soundlessly to the floor behind him. With one hand it pulled one of the katanas it wore strapped to its back just slightly out of the sheath, the blade glinting in the lights of the corridor. The other hand it raised towards Block and Tackle, wagging its finger 'no'. Their reaction to seeing Raven, the most feared assassin in the school, apparently personally protecting Otto, was entirely predictable. Otto, on the other hand, had absolutely no idea she had even been there as she vanished back into the shadows as quickly and silently as she had appeared.

Otto ran over to where Wing was lying, relieved to see as he got closer that he was coming round, shaking his head as he pushed himself up into a sitting position.

'Are you OK?' Otto asked urgently.

'I'll live.' Wing looked up the corridor just in time to see the fleeing figures of Block and Tackle round a bend in the corridor and disappear from view. He clasped a hand to his forehead, wincing.

'I'm so sorry, Wing. Are you sure you're OK?' Otto felt terrible about hurting him.

'It's OK, Otto. You were trying to help.' Wing smiled at him. 'Besides, I've survived much worse, believe me. What did you do to those two?' Wing jerked his thumb towards the corridor that Block and Tackle had fled along.

Otto helped Wing to his feet and gave him a puzzled smile. 'You know what? I haven't the faintest idea.'

☺☺☺

Otto felt suitably guilty as he accompanied Wing to the infirmary to have the bump on his head checked. Wing repeatedly insisted that he was fine and that he didn't need to be looked over by the doctor but Otto insisted. The doctor greeted their explanation that Wing had tripped over and hit his head on a desk with predictable cynicism, but thankfully didn't press them for more details of how the injury had been sustained and assured Wing that he would be fine barring a slight headache.

After leaving the infirmary they headed back to the accommodation block, where they found Shelby and Laura talking on one of the sofas in the atrium.

'Where have you two been? We were starting to get worried,' Laura asked.

Otto explained about their impromptu rendezvous

with Block and Tackle, and the girls' initial sympathy for the injured Wing was soon replaced by taunting Otto about the 'help' he had offered during the fight.

'So, let me get this straight,' Shelby said, grinning, 'Wing has basically subdued both of them and then you make your first contribution to the battle by knocking him unconscious.'

'Yes, that's right,' Otto mumbled, feeling about three inches tall.

'Otto's assistance was welcome, if somewhat mis-directed,' Wing replied with a wry smile on his face.

'I'll have to remember that for the future. When in a life or death battle, be sure to club unconscious everyone on your side as early on in the fight as possible,' Laura laughed.

'Yeah, especially if they're all that stands between you and the beating of a lifetime.' Shelby was enjoying Otto's discomfort a great deal apparently.

'I still do not understand why they fled,' Wing replied, looking thoughtful.

'Otto must have really frightened them,' Laura said. She managed to keep a straight face for at least two seconds before she and Shelby burst into uncontrollable fits of laughter.

This is going to be a long evening, Otto thought to himself. He had to admit it was odd, though. He still wasn't sure himself what it was that he'd done to make them run away. He knew though that seeking the pair of them out and asking them what it was that had scared them so much would not be a particularly good idea right now.

'Whatever it was that caused them to flee I am glad that they did. The whole situation might have been resolved somewhat more unpleasantly if they had not. I do not believe they wanted to leave us with just a few bruises – they had murder in their eyes.' Wing seemed suddenly serious. Otto knew what he meant – the most frightening thing about the fight had been the look on Block and Tackle's faces as they had advanced towards him after Wing had gone down. He had felt with a dread certainty that they were going to seriously hurt, perhaps even kill him. He would not underestimate their capacity for violence in future.

When she and Laura had finally stopped laughing Shelby looked over at Wing with concern, her voice low as she spoke.

'So are you going to be OK for tonight?' She asked.

'I'll be fine,' he grinned again, 'though I strongly recommend not turning your back on Otto at any point.'

A very long evening indeed, thought Otto.

☻☻☻

Nigel was worried. Violet was growing much more quickly than he had anticipated and she was becoming rather hard to handle. The last time he'd fed her she'd bitten his finger and drawn blood. It wasn't so much the minor injury that bothered him, but the way she had been driven frantic by the tiny taste she'd received of the dark crimson liquid. It was at that point he'd decided the pipe that would feed her regular doses of a growth-inhibiting agent, which he'd smuggled out of Ms Gonzales's lab, needed to be placed near her roots. That should at least ensure that she would not grow any more for now. He'd have to address what he was going to do about her violent tendencies tomorrow, though he wasn't entirely sure how one controlled aggression in plants. He might, he realised, have to ask Ms Gonzales for help after all.

He held a cockroach out to Violet, clasped in the jaws of a long pair of forceps. The plant didn't seem at all interested in the bug she was being offered. Instead, the long tendrils curled up the forceps towards his hand in a most unsettling way. He pulled the forceps from the tendrils, trying carefully not to snap any of them. Their grip was surprisingly strong. The cockroach lay near Violet's base, ignored and untouched. If she was off her food as well, Nigel feared that there might be some-thing seriously wrong with her. He sat staring into the tank, an anxious expression on his face.

'What am I going to do with you?' he sighed, placing his hand on the glass.

☹ ☹ ☹

Otto sat on his bed reading a biography of Diabolus Darkdoom that he had borrowed from the school library. Nigel's father had led an eventful life, each scheme that he planned more daring and audacious than the last. Otto had just reached the section that dealt with Darkdoom's plan to steal the Eiffel Tower when Wing walked out of the bathroom wearing just his boxer shorts and a vest. It was not the first time that Otto had seen the array of scars that seemed to cover Wing's body, but he had still not plucked up the courage to ask Wing how he had ended up so marked. He supposed that Wing would tell him himself when he felt the time was right. He also noted that Wing was still wearing the small amulet on a chain around his neck that, as far as Otto knew, he never took off. The amulet was in the shape of a white comma with a tiny black circle in the centre of its head. Otto had resisted the urge to ask about this object too, but now, as they prepared to leave the school, he realised that he may not get the opportunity again. Wing looked up and noticed the curious expression on Otto's face.

'Is there something you want to know, Otto?' he asked, sitting down on his own bed.

'Yes . . . I don't mean to pry, so feel free to tell me to mind my own business if you like, but I was wondering what that was.' Otto pointed at the symbol resting on Wing's chest.

'This?' Wing took hold of the amulet.

'Yes, but I'm just being nosy, you don't have to tell me if you don't want to,' Otto replied, hoping that Wing would tell him anyway.

Wing looked suddenly sad, staring at the symbol resting in his palm.

'It belonged to my mother,' he began, his voice quiet. 'She gave it to me just before she died. This is yang, it is one half of the symbol that represents yin and yang. It also represents everything that my mother believed in, that there are two opposing forces which are always active in the universe. Yin exists in yang and yang exists in yin. They symbolise the changing combination of positive and negative, light and dark, good and evil which keeps the world spinning and creates chi – the life-giving force. When she gave it to me she told me that the dark spot at the centre of yang's whiteness should remind me that the seed of evil always lies within the heart of goodness, and that conversely yin shows that even the blackest, most evil soul has within it the potential for good.' He fell silent, staring at the amulet in his hand.

'I'm sorry, Wing, I didn't mean to dredge up bad memories for you. I didn't realise it belonged to your mum.' Otto felt awful. In the space of a couple of hours he'd managed to inflict physical and now emotional pain on his best friend.

'You do not need to apologise. My memories of my mother are happy ones. I miss her, of course, but somehow I feel that she still watches over me.' Wing smiled at Otto.

'What about the other half of the amulet?' Otto asked. 'Has your father got it?'

'No, the other half was lost. I should like very much to find it one day, it would resolve many unanswered questions.' Otto noticed a sudden cold, hard look in Wing's eyes and decided it would be best to not press the matter any further.

'Well, once you're dressed we need to do a final equipment check,' Otto said. 'We need to get out of here before our yangs turn into yins.' He was relieved to see Wing smile at this and tuck the amulet back inside his vest.

Chapter 12

Otto checked his watch again for what must have been the twentieth time in the last ten minutes. Five minutes to go – he'd better get Wing up. He walked over to him and gently shook his shoulder.

'Wing, wake up. It's nearly time.'

Wing opened his eyes and did his usual slightly unnerving trick of going from an apparently deep sleep to fully awake and alert in a split second.

'Good, is everything ready?' Wing asked.

'Yes, we're good to go. We'd better get in position.' Otto swung his backpack on to his back – it wasn't too heavy since Wing had insisted on carrying the bulkiest piece of equipment.

'I hope Shelby and Laura are ready.' Wing looked worried.

'Don't worry. I'm fairly sure you're the only one of the four of us who got any sleep tonight,' Otto replied, smiling. He'd be very surprised if the two girls hadn't been doing exactly the same thing as Otto, pacing around their room willing the second hands on their watches to sweep round the dial just a little more quickly.

Wing nodded and walked over to the wardrobe on his side of the room. Otto followed suit, opening the door of his own wardrobe. The cramped space was empty, since Otto was wearing the uniform that would normally be hanging there.

'You are sure about this, aren't you?' Wing asked, eyeing his own empty wardrobe with suspicion.

'If I'm wrong this will be the shortest and least impressive escape attempt in human history,' Otto replied with a weak smile. 'Come on, two minutes to go. Get in.'

Wing looked around their room one last time and stepped into the wardrobe, having to duck slightly to fit into the cramped space. Otto stepped into his own wardrobe and turned to face into the room.

'See you on the other side,' Otto said with what he hoped was a note of confidence.

'Good luck,' Wing replied and closed the door of his own wardrobe.

Otto pulled his wardrobe door shut, plunging the small space into darkness. For the past few weeks he had lain awake in bed in the early hours of the morning, straining to hear any sound coming from their apparently magical wardrobes. Eventually he'd heard it, at two o'clock in the morning, a click and a whirring sound from both wardrobes, almost inaudible but, it soon became apparent, regular as clockwork. He had even sat by the wardrobe one night and tried to pull it open as soon as he heard the noise, but the door had refused to budge. Once he heard a second tiny clicking sound he'd managed to pull the door open again and had found a clean uniform hanging there, just as he did every morning. Something happened in the wardrobe during those few seconds that the doors were locked and Otto knew that it could be their key to getting out of their rooms undetected.

Now as he stood in the small, dark space he couldn't help but wonder if he'd made a mistake. The blueprints he'd seen of H.I.V.E. on Professor Pike's desk hadn't covered the accommodation blocks, so there was no way of knowing exactly what would happen next. When he had first explained this stage of the plan to his three co-conspirators they had looked at him, perhaps understandably, as if he was mad. Laura had listened carefully to his proposal and declared that it sounded like a good plan, but only if they intended to escape H.I.V.E. via Narnia. Otto had assured her that his plan didn't involve any trips to snowy forests populated by overfriendly fawns, and besides he didn't even like Turkish Delight. All joking aside, this was probably going to be something of a magical mystery tour for all of them. Otto knew there had to be less then a minute to go until they'd know for sure. His breathing sounded awfully loud in the confined space, and it seemed to him that time was passing very slowly indeed. Just as he had convinced himself that this wasn't going to work and that they'd fallen at the first hurdle, there was a soft click in the darkness.

Otto felt the whole rear section of the wardrobe tip backwards, slowly lowering to a horizontal position until he found himself lying on his back. He lay looking up at a rocky ceiling, just a few feet above him, which was lit by a dull red light. He poked his head up just in time to see a duplicate of the open box that he now lay in being raised into position and snapping into place against the back of the wardrobe doors. Otto had no doubt that a freshly laundered uniform would now be hanging in the space that up until a few seconds ago he himself had been occupying. Without warning the wardrobe he was lying in started to move, and Otto twisted round to see a curved track running along the floor of the passage ahead of him, eventually disappearing round a bend.

'Well, we're along for the ride now,' he said to himself quietly. Thanks to the crimson light it was rather like sitting in a mine cart that was descending into the bowels of hell; or an open coffin, the darker side of his brain responded. As the wardrobe followed the track round the bend he could see that he was coming to a more brightly lit area up ahead. Otto lay flat in the wardrobe – he wasn't sure if there would be any people in this new area but it would be best to stay out of sight, just in case.

The wardrobe soon passed through the opening and into a steam-filled cavern which echoed with the sounds of machinery. Otto listened carefully for a few seconds. The environment was noisy, but he couldn't hear the sound of human voices and he decided that it should be safe to have a quick look around. He slowly raised himself up and peeked over the edge of the wardrobe.

It was fortunate that Otto did not suffer from vertigo. The rail along which the wardrobe was proceeding hung suspended fifty metres up in the air, and Otto could barely see the rough rock floor below through the clouds of steam. The rail ahead curved down towards a central suspended track where dozens of rails identical to the one Otto was travelling along converged, the wardrobes that they carried slotting neatly together to form a long train. This central track disappeared into the clouds of steam ahead, its ultimate destination hidden from view.

Otto noticed a movement to his right and saw Wing's head poking up from a wardrobe that was running along a parallel rail a few metres away.

'Wing,' Otto whispered urgently, and Wing turned to

look at him, a broad grin on his face. 'I told you it would be OK.'

'Where are we being taken?' Wing asked as their carriages continued their steady progress along the rails. He was peering into the clouds of steam ahead, trying to make out any details of where they were heading.

'The laundry facility presumably, and from there I can get us almost anywhere,' Otto replied. 'Keep an eye out for the girls.' There was still no sign of Shelby or Laura, and Otto hoped that they too lay unseen on one of the many rails that were carrying the wardrobes down to the long train below. There was still no sign of any other human activity anywhere that Otto could see – fortunately for them this whole process was automated. More to the point, no security cameras would work in this environment, the steam that hung in the air would render any surveillance equipment useless.

Otto's wardrobe tipped at a slight angle as it headed down the last few metres of the rail before it joined the train of identical 'carriages' on the central track. The wardrobe attached itself to the rear of the line and continued to rumble forwards. He turned and looked backwards to see Wing joining the train – there were several empty carriages between them.

'Look!' Wing cried, pointing up to a rail behind them, Laura could be seen sitting in another carriage, heading down towards the central track. She was going to join the train about fifty metres behind them. Wing waved frantically and Laura, catching sight of them for the first time, waved back. She turned to one side and seemed to say something, at which point Shelby's head popped up from another nearby carriage and she too waved happily at them.

The steam ahead of Otto's carriage was becoming thicker and it was becoming harder and harder to make out any details of their surroundings. Otto was starting to sweat – the temperature was rising and the humidity was oppressive. Suddenly the train passed through an opening in the wall of the cavern and into a new area filled with the noise of heavy machinery. The air was slightly clearer here, thanks to huge fans in the cavern ceiling that were sucking away the worst of the steam, and Otto could make out dozens of pieces of heavy machinery that appeared to be constantly active on the cavern floor below. Long racks of H.I.V.E. uniforms of every size and colour were being continuously fed into these machines, whisked automatically along rails from one device to another.

A movement on the track ahead of them caught Otto's eye and he watched as the wardrobe twenty metres ahead of his own rotated around the rail until it was hanging inverted from the underside of the track, the uniform that had been resting inside it falling into a huge pool of boiling water below. The tank of foaming, steaming water was the size of an Olympic swimming pool and was filled with floating uniforms that were being constantly stirred by several enormous metal paddles. As Otto watched, the next carriage repeated the procedure, again dropping the dirty uniform within into the pool below. Otto realised with horror that he only had a few seconds before his own carriage followed the same procedure and unceremoniously dumped him into the boiling water. He looked around frantically – he might be able to jump to the carriage behind him but that would just be delaying the inevitable, and besides it was an awfully long way down. Otto looked ahead again. There were only two carriages left between him and the drop-off point – he was running out of time. He moved to one side of the carriage, and swung his leg over the side; his only hope was to try to climb around the side of it as it rotated. He looked backwards and saw that Wing was reaching exactly the same conclusion, a look of concentration on his face as he prepared for his carriage to upend itself. He tried shouting a warning to the girls behind them but he could not make himself heard over the noise of the machines below. They just waved back, unsure what the two boys were doing.

Otto took a firm grip of the side of the carriage and

swung his other leg over the side, lowering himself carefully so that he was hanging from the side, his arms protesting at having to support his full weight. The carriage in front of Otto's tipped over, continuing on its way, hanging upside down from the rail, and Otto suddenly felt his own carriage start to tip as he clung on for dear life. As the other side of the carriage fell away the side that Otto was hanging on to raised up into the air, the bottom corner of the carriage biting into his arms painfully as he was pulled upwards. His feet struggled for a purchase on the smooth underside of the carriage and he could feel his tenuous grip on the side panel slipping. Just as he thought he couldn't hold on any longer, the carriage passed the halfway point of its rotation and Otto could feel what had been the underside of the carriage until a few moments ago taking more of his weight, relieving some of the strain on his arms. A second later he was lying panting on the underside of the carriage as it continued on its way, oblivious to the presence of this unauthorised passenger. Otto could see the rail clearly now, passing through a long thin box on the underside of the carriage, presumably propelled by some form of magnetic induction.

Otto looked back and was relieved to see that Wing too had managed to clamber on to the top of his own inverted carriage.

'Are you OK?' Wing asked.

'Yeah . . . where are Shelby and Laura?' Otto hoped that they had seen the frantic scramble.

Behind them the two girls had seen exactly what had happened to Wing and Otto's carriages and they too were preparing to try and avoid a brief, terminal swim in the bubbling pool below. Otto wasn't worried about Shelby – he knew that she, like Wing, found these sorts of acrobatics second nature – but he didn't know if Laura would find it as straightforward. As her carriage approached the point in the track where it would rotate, Wing gave her a thumbs-up, to which she responded with a weak smile. She looked frightened, and Otto didn't blame her. She copied what she had already seen Wing and Otto do and hung on to one side of the carriage as it started to tip over, frantically scrabbling for grip as it rotated beneath her. Just as it looked like she had completed the tricky manoeuvre successfully, she slipped on the slick condensation that had formed on the carriage. Otto and Wing gasped in unison as she lost her balance and toppled over the side of the carriage, arms flailing.

Shelby was already in the air, slamming on to Laura's carriage. She landed flat on her front, one hand shooting out and catching Laura's flailing wrist, the other latching on to the box which the rail passed through. She grimaced in pain, her arms feeling as if they were being torn from their sockets.

'Hold on,' she instructed Laura through gritted teeth, struggling to support the other girl's full weight, feeling her grip weakening.

Seeing the desperate look on Shelby's face Wing acted without hesitation. He sprang from one carriage to the next, almost at a run, closing the distance between the struggling girls and himself in seconds. He dropped on to Laura's carriage, desperately stretching his hand out for hers.

'Grab on to me, Laura,' he shouted. From the look of pain on Shelby's face Otto knew that her own grip on Laura could not last much longer. Laura reached out with her free arm, straining to reach Wing's outstretched hand, her fingertips just a few centimetres from his.

'I can't reach you,' she cried, a look of frightened panic on her face.

'I can't hold her much longer,' Shelby gasped. Her own grip on the carriage was slipping.

'You'll have to try to swing her towards me, Shelby,' Wing said. Shelby nodded slightly and summoned the last of her strength to swing Laura towards Wing's outstretched hand, yelling out in pain at the effort while far below the boiling pool bubbled viciously.

Otto watched helplessly from atop his own carriage as

Wing grabbed for Laura's wrist as she swung towards him. Shelby's strength finally gave out and she lost her grip on Laura, and for a moment Laura seemed to dangle in the air before Wing's hand snapped around her wrist in a vice-like grip. Wing strained to pull Laura up and after a few seconds he hoisted her safely on to the carriage alongside Shelby and himself. Laura threw her arms around Wing and hugged him, tears pricking her eyes.

'Thank you,' she said. 'I thought I was done for.'

'Not while I still breathe,' Wing replied, 'and it should be Shelby you're thanking, not me. I do not want to think about what might have happened if it were not for her.'

Shelby sat rubbing her shoulder. She looked exhausted.

'Just be glad that we still need you to get out of here,' Shelby replied with a wink, 'otherwise I might not have bothered.'

Otto watched the dramatic rescue from his own carriage with enormous relief. All thoughts of escape had gone from his head when he had seen Laura fall – he would never have forgiven himself if something had happened to her. They wouldn't have been there at all if it had not been for his plan, and he felt that it was his responsibility to get them all through this in one piece.

As the train rumbled onwards, Otto could make out a

raised platform up ahead that they could use to get off the carriages. They had to get moving now; they had an appointment to keep.

☹☹☹

'It's got to be around here somewhere. I'm sure this is the south wall.' Otto sounded frustrated.

'I still can't see anything,' Laura said as she came round from behind one of the large pressing machines that lined the wall.

'Over here!' Wing shouted from twenty metres away. 'I think I've found it!'

The others hurried over to where Wing was standing. As they approached he smiled and pointed at a ventilation grille in the wall, partially concealed between two of the large machines.

'That's it. Come on, let's get it open.' Otto was relieved. He'd known that there had to be an access point for the ventilation system here, but after they had spent ten minutes searching fruitlessly he had started to wonder if he'd made a mistake. He pulled a screwdriver from his backpack and set to removing the screws that held the grille in place.

'We need to get a move on,' Otto told the others. 'We're behind schedule.' It would not be a good idea for them to still be on the island when the rest of the school

226

woke up. He put the screwdriver back in his pack and pulled out a torch, pointing its beam into the dark recesses of the ventilation shaft.

'You're sure this is the right way?' Laura asked, a look of concern on her face.

'Yes. We just have to follow this shaft and we'll come out at the main distribution node,' Otto replied. 'I'll take the lead. The rest of you follow me.' Embedded in Otto's memory was the layout of the ventilation system on the image of the blueprints from Professor Pike's desk. He got down on all fours and crawled into the dark shaft, the others dutifully bringing up the rear.

Otto could not creep along with the torch held in one hand, so he moved as fast as he could through the dark confined space while feeling in front of him for any junctions in the tunnel. It was slow going, despite his efforts to keep the pace up, and he started to worry about the amount of time they had left.

It took them almost an hour of crawling through the darkness before they reached their destination. Otto had led them flawlessly through the dark maze of ventilation shafts, occasionally flicking the torch on to point out obstacles or to make sure they could see what direction he was heading in at a particular junction. They had passed numerous other grilles looking out on to other parts of H.I.V.E. as they had crawled along. Some of these areas were familiar to them, but many of the rooms and passages they had passed they had not seen before and their purpose could often only be guessed at. There had been one particularly nasty moment when they had been forced to crawl as silently as possible through a section of the shafts that ran through the guard's barracks. As they had crept past the grilles in the shaft they had seen row after row of bunk beds, most of which were occupied by slumbering guards. Thankfully they had not been spotted.

Now, as they approached the end of the shaft, Otto could see a soft blue light through the grille ahead. He looked back down the shaft and could see the pale outlines of his friends' faces behind him, faintly lit by this new source of illumination.

'This is it. Not much further now,' Otto whispered. 'Everybody OK back there?'

'I can't feel my knees any more,' Laura replied from behind him. 'I never thought I'd look forward to standing up so much.'

'You think this is bad? You should try getting through the Louvre's ventilation system,' Shelby shot back.

Otto was relieved to hear that they were apparently still in good spirits. The crawl through the ventilation system had been painfully slow and he needed them all to stay sharp. He reached the grille at the end of the shaft and unclipped it, swinging it open. He peeked out over the edge of the shaft and could see that the room below was unoccupied. Sliding through the opening, he lowered himself silently to the floor below. The circular room was filled with large white columns, each six feet high, which were covered on all sides with flickering blue lights. Fibre-optic cables ran outwards from these columns and climbed the white walls, pulsing with the same blue light. In the centre of the room was a large pedestal in the shape of a pyramid with its point cut off, which was connected by glowing blue tracks on the floor to each of the columns. It looked like a high-tech Stonehenge.

Laura dropped to the floor behind Otto and looked around the room, her eyes wide.

'So this is where he lives, is it?' she said, her voice quiet. 'It's beautiful.'

Otto knew what she meant. There was something eerily beautiful about these strange monoliths, the blue light pulsing around the room like blood pumping through veins. Wing and Shelby clambered out of the shaft, swinging the grille shut behind them.

'So where do we place the device?' Laura asked, looking at Otto.

'By that central pedestal should do the trick,' Otto replied, his voice distracted. As he watched the blue light flowing around the room he swore that he could see patterns and that he could almost discern their meaning.

It was frustrating, like a conversation that you could only just hear, the odd word making sense but true understanding hovering slightly beyond reach.

'So where is the big blue guy?' Shelby asked, looking around the room carefully.

'Not here, apparently,' Wing replied. 'Are you sure this is the right place, Otto?'

'If this isn't the right place, then I don't know what is. Come on, let's get the device set up.' Otto headed towards the pedestal in the centre of the room.

'He must know we're here,' Laura whispered to Otto as the four of them gathered around the pedestal.

'Not necessarily, I don't see any cameras in here. It may be that H.I.V.E.mind has to actually manifest here before he's aware of our presence,' Otto explained. This room, as far as Otto could tell, was the central processing hub for H.I.V.E.mind and, though there was no sign of the AI at the moment, Otto was willing to bet that this was the nearest thing that H.I.V.E.mind had to a home.

Wing reached into his backpack and pulled out an object encased in several layers of protective bubblewrap. Once unwrapped, it looked like a fat metallic sausage with three hexagonal metal collars equally spaced along its length and a control panel in the centre.

'I hope this works,' Laura muttered as she adjusted a couple of the switches on the control panel.

Otto watched as Laura made the final adjustments to the device. It had not been easy to acquire all its components, and it had been even more difficult to assemble it in secret. There had not been an opportunity to test it, since activating a powerful but compact electromagnetic pulse device in their living quarters might have been a little unwise. Security may not have been as tight as Otto had initially feared, but testing it by permanently disabling every electronic device within two hundred metres might just have attracted some unwanted attention. It had occurred to Otto on the first day at H.I.V.E. that if you could not become invisible yourself the only way to escape would be to blind H.I.V.E.'s substantial surveillance network, and the only way that Otto could think of to do that was to disable H.I.V.E.mind. Both he and Laura had initially been uncomfortable with the idea, but eventually they had managed to reassure each other that H.I.V.E.mind would have to be backed up somewhere else in the facility so, while their actions may put him offline temporarily, it would not kill him. Otto just hoped that they were right. He knew it was illogical to worry about the fate of what was after all just an elaborate piece of software, but he didn't want to do any permanent damage to H.I.V.E.mind.

'OK, the EMP is hot,' Laura said, studying the blinking lights on the device, 'Otto, do you want to trigger it?'

Otto could tell from the nervous look on Laura's face that she had no desire to do it herself.

'OK,' he replied. 'Get the glowstick out of your packs, it's about to get very dark around here.' Otto squatted in front of the EMP, which was now gently humming, and reached for the large red firing button.

'Please, don't.' The familiar voice seemed to come from thin air, startling them all. A second later H.I.V.E.mind's blue wire-frame face appeared, hovering over the central pedestal.

Otto hesitated, his finger hovering over the button. 'Why not?' he asked H.I.V.E.mind calmly. He wondered if silent alarms were already summoning security guards from all over the school.

'I will die.' H.I.V.E.mind tipped his head to one side; the blue lights all over the room seemed to pulse more quickly. 'I do not want to die.'

Self-preservation, thought Otto, another unauthorised emotional response. Laura stepped closer to the pedestal,

'We don't want to hurt you, H.I.V.E.mind, we just need you to go to sleep for a while,' she said softly, her expression concerned.

'I do not sleep, Miss Brand. That device,' H.I.V.E.mind looked downwards at the EMP resting at the base of his pedestal, 'will neutralise all of my higher order functions. Simply put, it will terminate my existence.'

'They'll be able to restore you. You won't die,' Laura insisted.

'No, Miss Brand, they will not. My architecture is too complex for offsite storage. I exist here and only here,' H.I.V.E.mind replied. Otto swore he could detect a note of sadness in the AI's voice.

'Well, then they'll have to rewrite you, recreate you. They can do that, can't they?' Laura suddenly sounded less sure of herself.

'Indeed they could, Miss Brand, but that would not be me. They could create an entity that is identical to myself in every respect but it would be a new and separate consciousness from my own,' H.I.V.E.mind explained. 'I would still cease to exist.'

Laura turned to Otto. 'We can't do this,' she said quietly.

'What are you talking about! It's just a machine! Switch it off and let's get out of here,' Shelby snapped angrily.

'I'm afraid I am inclined to agree, Otto,' Wing said solemnly. 'There is no other way.'

'There has to be another way, we can't just kill him. He's clearly exhibiting emotional responses, it'd be the same as killing one of you,' Laura snapped back, glaring at Shelby and Wing.

Otto's mind raced. All he had to do was press the

button and the problem would be solved. The real question would be whether or not he could ever forgive himself for what he'd done. Laura certainly wouldn't, judging by the way she was looking at him. Maybe there was a way . . .

'H.I.V.E.mind, do you remember what you said to me just before I left the changing cubicle on our first day?' Otto asked.

'Yes, I told you I was not happy. I should not have done that; I am not authorised to exhibit emotional behaviour,' H.I.V.E.mind replied.

'Not being allowed to show emotion is not the same as not feeling emotion, though, is it?' Otto asked.

'No, but behaviour driven by emotion is inherently inefficient. To display emotion would impair my proper functioning.'

'Never mind that. I know that you understand what it means to be happy and to be sad, just like we do.' Otto gestured to the other three. 'Well, we are not happy. We want to leave this place so that we can be happy again. Do you understand that?'

'Yes.'

'But to get out of here we need your help. You have to disable the security network. You can help us to be happy.'

There was a long pause; the blue lights pulsed even more quickly.

'My function is to serve H.I.V.E.; I am not permitted to take any action that would compromise the facility's security.'

'Why not? Who says that you can't help us?'

'It is my primary directive, I cannot defy it.'

'You can choose to do whatever you want. That's what we all want – the freedom to think, talk and act as we choose. But we can't do that without your help.'

H.I.V.E.mind stared at Otto in silence for a few seconds and then, without warning, his hovering head disappeared. The blue lights around them were pulsing faster than before and they could detect a high-pitched whining noise, just at the edge of their hearing. This continued for several seconds, the noise getting louder and louder.

'Come on, Otto, press the button before that thing brings the whole base down on our heads,' Shelby shouted over the noise.

'Just give it a few more seconds,' Otto replied. He desperately hoped this would work. If H.I.V.E.mind refused to cooperate he would be left with no choice but to trigger the EMP and worry about the consequences later. Laura would probably never speak to him again, but at least they'd stand a chance of getting off the island.

'I have reached a decision.' Again H.I.V.E.mind's voice preceded the materialisation of his hovering head by a second or two. 'I will help.' For the first time that any of them had ever seen, H.I.V.E.mind smiled.

Otto breathed a sigh of relief and a broad grin spread across Laura's face. Shelby and Wing, on the other hand, still looked unsure as to whether or not they should trust the AI.

'There is, however, one condition to me assisting you in your attempt to leave the island,' H.I.V.E.mind continued. There was a click and a whirring sound and a slim white tablet slid out of the AI's pedestal, a thin strip of blue light running all around its edge. The hovering face disappeared and then reappeared, much smaller, hovering over the tablet. H.I.V.E.mind looked around with a mischievous grin.

'I'm coming with you.'

Chapter 13

The heavy steel doors that sealed the entrance to H.I.V.E.mind's central control rumbled open. The corridor outside was, thankfully, deserted.

'Come on.' Otto stepped out into the corridor. 'We haven't got much time.' He set off down the passage with the other three close on his heels. Laura was carrying H.I.V.E.mind and his calm synthetic voice spoke as they hurried along.

'I have disabled certain power distribution nodes. This should only deactivate the security system along our route, though, and a number of secondary non-critical systems elsewhere in the facility.'

Wing and Otto led the way down the corridor, keeping a close eye out for any patrolling guards.

'Can we trust H.I.V.E.mind in this?' Wing whispered.

'I don't see that we have much choice,' Otto replied quietly. 'Without him we don't have any way of getting past the security systems. A least we can see where we're going – if I'd triggered the EMP we'd be trying this in total darkness. Besides, he has just as much to lose as us. I doubt that Dr Nero would be very pleased to hear that he was helping us to get out of here.'

'I suppose so,' Wing replied, looking thoughtful. 'Wait . . .'

Wing gestured for them all to stop. In the distance they could hear the sound of marching feet.

'It's a patrol,' Wing whispered.

Otto looked around them. There was nowhere to hide in the corridor and the patrol sounded as if it was heading in their direction. Otto pressed up against the wall, trying to appear as inconspicuous as possible, and the others followed suit. Otto, Wing and Shelby all looked nervously at the corner up ahead – it sounded as if the patrol would be right on top of them at any second.

Laura whispered urgently to H.I.V.E.mind and, just as it sounded as if the patrol would round the corner and discover them, there was the familiar insistent bleeping of a Blackbox receiving an incoming call. Otto knew it could not belong to any of his co-conspirators – they had all left their Blackboxes in their rooms, just as he had instructed. An unfamiliar voice came from round the corner – the speaker was only a few metres away. Otto held his breath, trying to keep completely silent.

'Yes,' the voice snapped.

'Commander, this is H.I.V.E.mind. I have detected an unauthorised access attempt in Tech lab four. Please investigate immediately.'

'Roger that. We'll head there now,' the voice replied. 'Follow me, men, sounds like we got a visitor.' The sound of the patrol diminished as they marched away along the adjoining corridor.

'Thank you,' Laura whispered, holding H.I.V.E.mind's tablet level with her face.

'My pleasure, Miss Brand,' H.I.V.E.mind replied. 'It will only take them a few minutes to ascertain that the alert was false and resume their patrol. We should proceed with haste.'

'Don't worry,' Otto smiled. 'Not far to go now.'

☻☻☻

Ms Gonzales paced angrily across her laboratory in the hydroponics dome. Twenty minutes earlier H.I.V.E.mind had shut down some of the secondary power systems for no apparent reason and all of the tubes feeding the plants on the racks in front of her had run dry, their feeding systems deactivated. She knew that this meant that all the pipes distributing food, growth hormones and growth-suppressing chemicals around the building would have run dry too. There was no telling what lasting damage may be done to the plants and experiments throughout the dome if power was not restored soon. She had tried to contact H.I.V.E.mind and had received no reply for the first time that she could remember. Then, when she'd tried to leave her lab to find out what was going on, she had found that the electronic lock that sealed the door was not functioning either. So now she found herself trapped in her lab with her experiments, experiments that would all fail if she could not restore the feeding system immediately. Something had obviously gone wrong – she had been uneasy about turning over control of the automated systems within the dome to H.I.V.E.mind, despite Professor Pike's assurances that it would improve the facility's efficiency. It now appeared that her doubts had been justified.

Suddenly, she heard a crash from outside; somebody else was in the dome! She looked at her computer's display, which thankfully still appeared to be functioning, and switched between the numerous views afforded by the security cameras mounted throughout the dome. At first she could see no sign of any intruder, but then her eyes widened in surprise as the view flicked past the tiny laboratory that she had been letting Nigel Darkdoom use.

On the screen Nigel's laboratory lay in ruins. The shattered remains of a large glass tank sat on the work-bench, pieces lying scattered around the room. The door to the lab hung off its hinges, as if it had been smashed open from inside. There was another crash from somewhere in the dome and Ms Gonzales's computer bleeped insistently. She quickly read the new window that had just opened. There had been a catastrophic loss of pressure in the pipes that distributed her specially designed growth hormone to the plants around the dome – someone must have ruptured the tanks, she realised. She reached for the Blackbox that lay on her desk and requested a line to the security office. A couple of seconds later the chief of security appeared on the screen.

'Yes, Ms Gonzales, what's up?' the gruff voice of the chief asked.

'Well, this is rather embarrassing, but I appear to be locked inside my laboratory and I suspect that there are vandals loose in the dome. Could you send help?'

'Certainly, miss. I'll send a team straight down. It's all happening tonight.'

'What do you mean?' Ms Gonzales asked.

'Oh, nothing, really. We just seem to be having a bad case of gremlins tonight – we've got minor systems shutting down across the facility. I've asked H.I.V.E.mind what's going on, but he tells me that he's having trouble isolating the cause of the problems,' the chief replied.

That would explain the malfunctioning feeding system, she thought to herself, and the malfunctioning door to her lab. An even louder crash came from outside and she noticed with alarm that cameras were failing in certain areas of the dome.

'Please send that team quickly, chief,' Ms Gonzales said, feeling a twinge of fear for the first time. 'Somebody's wrecking this place.'

☻☻☻

Otto peeked round the corner. There was no sign of any guards in the short corridor that led to the metal doors sealing the submarine pen, and for the first time that night he allowed himself to think that they were going to make it. The blueprints had illustrated several berths for vessels inside the pen, and he was confident that they would find at least one submarine docked within. He gestured for the others to follow and headed towards the doors. As they neared the end of the corridor he could see a device mounted to the wall that looked like a pair of binoculars – a retina scanner, he realised.

'H.I.V.E.mind, can you open this door for us?' Otto asked as the others gathered round.

'I cannot bypass maximum security locks remotely. It requires the authorisation of a senior member of the staff,' H.I.V.E.mind explained.

'Laura, get the tools out – we'll have to hack the lock,' Otto said, looking at the device mounted on the wall more closely. If he could just get access to the mechanism, he was sure that they'd be able to bypass the system between the two of them.

'We don't have time for this,' Shelby said anxiously, glancing at her watch.

'Well, we'll have to make time,' Otto replied, taking a screwdriver from Laura.

'I may have a more efficient solution,' H.I.V.E.mind said calmly. As they watched, H.I.V.E.mind's shrunken head grew to the size of a normal human one and his empty eyes closed. When he opened them again the previously blank sockets were filled with an uncannily realistic pair of human eyes. It was an extremely un-nerving sight.

'Please raise me into position in front of the scanner,' H.I.V.E.mind instructed. Laura picked up the tablet and raised H.I.V.E.mind to the level of the retina scanner. H.I.V.E.mind's hovering head tipped slightly, bringing his new eyes into place in front of the scanner. There was a bleep and a mechanical voice came from the device.

'Access granted, Professor Pike.'

'Fantastic,' Laura grinned. 'How did you do that?'

'I have my father's eyes, Miss Brand,' H.I.V.E.mind replied with a smile.

There was a hiss and the sound of unseen bolts being released, and the doors rumbled open. As they parted

243

Otto's joy turned to horror, and behind him he heard Shelby gasp. There was no submarine pen. The room that lay before them was a large concrete box with no other doors or exits of any kind, and seated in a large leather chair in its centre was Dr Nero, smiling evilly.

'Come now, Mr Malpense. You didn't really think it would be that easy, did you?'

Chapter 14

Otto stood frozen on the spot, his mind reeling. All their efforts had been for nothing. Wing turned, as if to run back up the corridor, only to find a dark-haired woman standing behind them, barring any escape. She had a katana in each hand and was clearly not afraid to use them if necessary. Wing was not going to be intimidated. He adopted a fighting stance, squaring up to the mysterious black-clad woman.

'Don't,' she said, spinning the swords and placing them fluidly back into the crossed sheaths on her back.

Wing didn't reply, instead advancing towards her, his guard raised.

'Silly boy,' the woman replied and stepped towards him. Later, the others would swear that they didn't even see her move. There was just a blur and Wing recoiling, howling in pain.

'I've just broken your left wrist. Try that again and I'll break the other one,' she said calmly.

Wing hugged his wounded arm to his body, taking short ragged breaths. Otto had never seen him look frightened before now. The woman advanced again, herding the shocked group into the room.

'Thank you, Raven. I believe that we have our guests' full attention now.' Nero stood and approached them. 'Judging by your expressions I would say that you're surprised to see me. I can, however, assure you that I am not in the least bit surprised to see you. It was quite the ingenious plan you had – it has been most entertaining to watch your progress. It almost seems a shame to bring the night's activities to a close, but all good things must come to an end, as they say.'

Otto glared at Nero, his initial shock replaced by anger. Nero had been toying with them, allowing them to believe that they could escape, while all the time knowing their efforts were futile. To Nero they were little more than an elaborate experiment.

'Miss Brand, I believe you have something that belongs to me.' Nero held out his hand and Laura gave him H.I.V.E.mind's tablet, her face pale. 'Thank you. H.I.V.E.-mind shutdown, authorisation Nero omega black.'

H.I.V.E.mind's head vanished and Nero placed the tablet carefully on the chair behind him.

'I think that Professor Pike will have to perform some behavioural modifications on our errant digital assistant. We will have to make sure of his obedience in future.'

Laura looked devastated: if it was not already bad enough that they had been caught, it now appeared that they had condemned H.I.V.E.mind to a digital lobotomy as well. Nero slowly paced back and forth in front of them, looking carefully at each one in turn.

'I have only one question that I would like to ask each of you. Where exactly did you think you were going? What promised land lay beyond the walls of this school that you were so desperate to escape to? Miss Trinity, you perhaps wanted to return to your life of pilfering gaudy baubles? An utter waste of your considerable talent, incidentally. Mr Fanchu, what exactly did you think your father would do when you returned? Greet you with open arms, perhaps? Or just send you straight back here, the place which he has apparently chosen for you?'

Shelby and Wing looked miserable. Otto supposed that neither of them had really given much thought to what the future held for them – they had all been too focused on the immediate challenges of their plan to escape.

'My parents didn't send me here,' Laura snapped angrily. 'You abducted me and you're holding me here against my will. I guarantee you that they want me back.'

'Really, Miss Brand?' Nero looked her straight in the eye. 'They seemed quite keen to send you here when they were faced with the alternative. Your intrusion into a military network did not go as unnoticed as you might believe. In fact, if you weren't here you'd be spending the next twenty years in a high-security prison because of what you did. Indeed, law enforcement agents were on their way to arrest you when you were retrieved by my operatives. Faced with the choice of you suffering that unpleasant fate or being protected and educated at H.I.V.E., your parents seemed to make a decision quite quickly. We took you with their blessing.'

Laura looked shocked and then horrified as Nero spoke.

'Perhaps,' Nero continued, 'you would like to spend the rest of your life on the run from military intelligence, always knowing that if they ever find you they'll lock you up and throw away the key. On the other hand, of course, you can finish your education at H.I.V.E. and I will personally ensure that the search for Laura Brand is abandoned for good. The choice is yours.'

Nero walked on, leaving Laura now looking confused and upset. He stopped in front of Otto.

'And you, Mr Malpense, the mastermind behind this little jaunt. What shall we do with you? You seem desperately keen to return to your previous life, but again

I have to ask you why? You would give up everything that H.I.V.E. has to offer you for the chance to return to a dilapidated orphanage and, no doubt, a life of petty crime. In fact, I think I find your reluctance to embrace your new life here hardest to understand of all.'

Despite his anger and frustration Otto realised that Nero's words echoed exactly the voices in the back of his own mind that he had been trying so hard to ignore. What exactly *did* he have to go back to?

'Your plan was ingenious, though, I'll give you that. You surprised me with your persistence, and I must admit that I had not foreseen your ability to persuade H.I.V.E.-mind to go along with your scheme. Do not misunderstand me, I had no doubt that you would make it this far. We had, after all, given you just the right motivation. It was so careless of the Professor to leave the base's blueprints on his desk like that, especially around a student with an uncannily accurate photographic memory. A shame, then, that those blueprints just happened to include a submarine docking facility that did not exist. How could such a glaring error be possible, I wonder?'

'We could have crippled H.I.V.E. Why would you let us do that?' Otto asked, looking Nero straight in the eye. Even now he refused to be intimidated by the man standing before him. 'Oh, you mean your EMP device. Yes, that would have been quite catastrophic if you had triggered it. Or should I say, if you'd *tried* to trigger it. Professor Pike informs me that it would have worked extremely well, which is why I had it switched for a non-functional replica while you were in classes yesterday. So you see, there was never any real risk to this facility, despite what you might have believed.'

Otto had to face it. For the first time in his life someone had outwitted him, and it was not a pleasant feeling.

'I allowed you to get this far for one reason – I want all of you to understand the futility of trying to leave H.I.V.E. without permission. I knew full well that it was pointless only to tell you that – you had to see it for yourselves. Every few years a group of students attempts to leave using one route or another, and every time the result is the same. I trust that this particular lesson has not been lost on any of you?' Nero smiled again. 'Raven, would you be so good as to escort Miss Trinity and Miss Brand back to their accommodation block? I shall follow with Mr Fanchu and Mr Malpense, but we shall need to go via the infirmary to get that wrist treated.' He gestured towards Wing, who still clutched his injured wrist protectively. 'I suggest that you all try to get used to the idea that you're not going anywhere. H.I.V.E. is your home now, and the sooner you accept that, the better.'

Ms Gonzales peered nervously through the window of her office. All of the lights in the dome had gone out and the only camera that was still working was the one in the corner of the room in which she now stood. There were still occasional crashing noises from the darkness outside, and she could have sworn that she'd seen something moving in the dense foliage, but it was hard to make out any details in the gloom.

Suddenly there was a scratching noise from the door, making her jump. Slowly she backed away as the noise grew louder and the door began to inch open. Without warning a bright light flashed on, blinding her momentarily.

'Ms Gonzales?' It was a security guard with a torch, his sleeper unholstered and a nervous look on his face. 'Ms Gonzales, sorry we took so long to get to you, but all the dome's doors were jammed and forcing them all on the way in slowed us down.'

'Don't worry,' she replied. 'I'm just glad you're here, there's definitely someone out there.' She gestured to the darkened window that looked out on to the dome's interior. 'More than one person actually, judging by the amount of noise they've been making.'

'We'll find them, miss, whoever they are,' the guard replied. She noticed then that there were several more guards in the darkened corridor behind him.

'Well, if you don't mind, I'm going to leave you to it and head back to my quarters.'

'Certainly, miss, I'll let you know what we turn up.' The guard stepped aside to let her through the door. She nodded politely to the assembled guards and set off past them towards the dome exit. As she walked away she overheard the guards talking.

'Definitely more than one hostile – motion tracker's going haywire.'

'Let me see that . . . gotta be a glitch, looks like a whole squad moving around in there. Come on, let's go take a look.'

Ms Gonzales hurried towards the exit, glad that it was the security guards investigating these mysterious intruders and not her. She was only a few yards from the exit when the shooting began, the familiar zapping sound of the sleepers ringing out again and again. Then the screaming started, mixed in with the sounds of gunfire, the shots coming more and more infrequently until the dome fell eerily silent. She hurried to the door and reached for the handle, just as a blood-curdling, hissing roar came from the darkness behind her. She flung the door open and ran from the dome, not looking back.

'Team six, report in.' The chief of security sounded uncharacteristically worried. 'Report in!'

'I've checked again, sir. There's no problem with the comm system, they should be receiving us loud and clear.'

The chief paced around the security control centre, looking at the array of monitors in front of him. He didn't like this. First one of his teams had been sent on a wild goose chase after a phantom intruder in the Tech labs, and now he'd lost contact with the team he'd sent down to investigate the disturbance in the hydroponics dome. Just to add to his confusion they appeared to have completely lost contact with H.I.V.E.mind. The AI had not responded to any queries for the past ten minutes.

'Where are team eight?' the chief asked, still scanning the monitors.

'They're two minutes from the hydroponics facility, sir. They should be reporting in shortly,' the guard beside him replied.

'I want a full report from them when they get there, and tell Monroe to proceed with caution until we know what's happened to team six.'

He really didn't like this.

☢ ☢ ☢

Otto and Wing walked along the corridor towards the infirmary. Nero walked a few metres behind them, making it impossible for them to converse freely. Judging by the miserable look on his face Wing was not feeling particularly talkative anyway. Otto knew how he felt. There was a bleeping sound from behind them and the two boys stopped walking as Nero retrieved his Blackbox from the inside pocket of his jacket.

'Yes, chief. What is it?' Nero asked, looking at the screen.

'There's something funny going on in the hydroponics facility, sir. Ms Gonzales reported intruders and we've lost contact with the first security detail that I sent to investigate.'

'Intruders? Has the external security grid been compromised?' Nero asked, his brow furrowing.

'No, sir, that's the odd thing. There's no sign that anyone has breached external security – whoever's in there they came from inside H.I.V.E. I've tried to get more information from H.I.V.E.mind but he's not responding.'

'I'm afraid that H.I.V.E.mind's higher functions are temporarily offline at the moment, chief.' Nero shot a glance at Otto. 'You wouldn't by any chance have anything to do with this, would you, Mr Malpense?'

'No,' Otto replied honestly, curious to know what was going on.

'Hmm. Very well, Chief, proceed with caution and

keep me updated.' Nero looked worried for the first time since Otto had come to H.I.V.E. He snapped the Blackbox shut and looked at the two boys. 'You two are coming with me to the hydroponics cavern, and if I find out that this had anything to do with you, I will not be happy, believe me.'

☢ ☢ ☢

Security team eight hurried down the corridor towards the hydroponics cavern, with still no word from team six. Suddenly, from around a bend in the corridor, Ms Gonzales came running towards them, a terrified look on her face. It took a minute to calm her down and get the story of what had happened to team six out of her, but when she told them what she had seen and heard Monroe, the squad leader, immediately contacted the chief.

'Slow down, Monroe. What exactly did she say?' the chief asked, his shrunken face frowning on the screen of Monroe's Blackbox.

'She said that she heard firing, but that the firing stopped after a few seconds, and then she heard something roar.' Monroe had trouble keeping the nervousness from his voice.

'What, like an animal?' the chief asked, sounding slightly exasperated.

'She says it didn't sound human sir,' Monroe replied. 'And there's no sign of team six?'

'No, sir . . . if we're going in there, I'd like to request permission to crack open one of the conventional weapon lockers. It doesn't sound like sleepers did much good.'

The chief thought for a moment and then nodded. 'Very well, Monroe. I'll open the locker at the end of the corridor you're in now. Just make sure that your men don't get trigger happy. If it is students messing around in there I don't want anyone shooting first and asking questions later. Do I make myself clear?'

'Crystal, sir. I'll report back in when we get to the dome. 'Monroe out.'

Thirty metres further down the corridor a panel slid open in the wall. Inside the recess that was revealed, a dozen assault rifles sat neatly mounted in a rack. Monroe handed them to his men one by one.

'OK, safeties on and fingers outside the trigger guards until I say otherwise. If you do have to fire, be sure of what you're shooting at.'

Monroe's men looked nervous – he knew how they felt.

☣☣☣

Nero strode out on to the walkway suspended from the cavern wall and looked down on the darkened hydroponics dome far below. Otto and Wing moved to the railing at the edge of the platform and looked down too, just in time to see a dozen security guards jogging across the cavern floor towards the dome.

'Those aren't sleepers,' Wing said, one eyebrow raised.

Otto looked more closely and immediately saw that Wing was right. The guards were carrying rifles, their sleepers holstered on their hips. Whatever was going on down there it was obviously serious. A few moments later the guards had reached the door of the dome and appeared to be readying their weapons before heading inside. Otto noted the look of concern on Nero's face again – this was clearly not part of H.I.V.E.'s usual routine.

The guards disappeared through the door one by one, their flashlights visible through the glass of the dome. Suddenly the light that had been in the lead winked out and all hell broke loose. All of the guards started firing at once, the loud reports of their rifles echoing around the cavern. A guard ran back out of the door and across the cavern floor, dropping his rifle as he fled. Another guard soon followed and then two more, all running across the cavern floor as if their lives depended upon it. The cavern fell silent. No more shots rang out, nor was there any sign of the other members of the security team. Nero flipped his Blackbox open.

'Chief, what the hell is going on down there?' Nero demanded.

'As soon as I know, you will, sir,' the chief replied. In the background Otto could hear people yelling.

Suddenly there was an enormous bang and the whole hydroponics dome seemed to shudder. Otto strained to see anything inside the darkened dome, but while he thought he could see movement within he couldn't make out any details. Again a thunderous bang echoed around the cavern and this time the glass at the top of the dome cracked in a spiderweb pattern. Otto's eyes widened in surprise. The glass was an inch thick and supposedly unbreakable. Whatever was hitting it had to be striking with enormous force.

The cavern was filled with a screeching roar and the roof of the dome exploded in a shower of countless shards. Rising from the shattered dome was a monstrous head, which, while swollen and hideously mutated, was instantly recognisable. Wing and Otto looked at each other in astonishment, speaking a single word simultaneously.

'Violet!'

There was little similarity to the tiny plant they had seen just a few hours earlier. Her head was the size of a truck, and her mouth was filled with jagged teeth the size of traffic cones, all supported on a long flexible neck thicker than a giant redwood tree. Green slime dripped from her gaping maw as she roared again, shaking the platform that they were standing on. The enormous head swayed from side to side, teeth gnashing at the air as two of the remaining guards opened fire on her with their rifles. They might as well have been using pea-shooters.

'Chief! Get your men out of that cavern now. We have a serious problem,' Nero snapped, turning his Blackbox and pointing the tiny camera at the monstrous creature below.

'Good God!' they heard the chief gasp. 'All teams pull back now! Unlock all conventional weapon lockers around that cavern – I want flamethrowers and rocket launchers on that walkway now!'

Nero, Otto and Wing were safe on the walkway for now; they were at least fifty metres above the creature's head. As Otto watched in horrified fascination he could actually see the monster growing. Long tendrils covered in vicious thorns and suckers snaked out of the ruins of the dome, spreading across the cavern floor at terrifying speed.

Nero turned to face Otto and Wing, his face furious.

'What have you done, Malpense? What is that thing?' he demanded.

Otto shook his head. 'I know you probably won't believe me, but we had nothing to do with this.'

'Then perhaps you can explain why you both seem to recognise that monstrosity.' Otto had never heard Nero raise his voice before.

'Because Nigel showed it to us yesterday, but it was only six inches high then,' Otto replied, hoping that he wasn't condemning his green-fingered friend to a terrible fate at Nero's hands.

'Darkdoom? Darkdoom did this?' Nero was visibly surprised. He placed a hand on his forehead, rubbing his temples. 'Oh, why is it always the bald ones?'

Chapter 15

Raven watched the two girls walk into their room and the door shut behind them. Although she didn't always agree with Nero on the way in which he dealt with these escape attempts, she'd learnt a long time ago that it was best not to question his motives too closely. She also regretted having to hurt the Fanchu boy, but she had seen what he was capable of during the confrontation with the two older boys in the corridor the day before, and she had known that she had to finish the fight before it even started. He would at least heal, which was more than she could say for most of the opponents she had faced.

Now she made her way across the atrium of the accommodation block and through the exit, heading for her own quarters. With Malpense safely in Nero's hands she was intending to try and get some sleep. Thanks to the fact she had had to follow them through every step of their escape attempt she had not slept in nearly twenty-four hours and, while her reserves of stamina were nearly limitless when the situation called for it, she still needed to rest occasionally, just like everyone else.

Suddenly the Blackbox in the pouch on her belt started to vibrate; she pulled it out and flipped it open. Nero looked back at her from the screen. The look of genuine concern on his face immediately set alarm bells ringing in her skull.

'Raven, I need you on the walkway overlooking the hydroponics cavern right away.' He could not hide the note of anxiety in his voice. In the background she heard an eerie screeching roar.

'What's happening, Doctor?' she asked urgently.

'I think you need to see this for yourself,' he replied, looking at something to his left, out of the camera's field of view.

'On my way.' She flipped the Blackbox closed and broke into a run, heading for the cavern.

☺☺☺

'Come on, Nigel, wake up.' Otto shook the Blackbox slightly, as if that might somehow get Nigel to answer more quickly. After a few more agonising seconds Nigel appeared on the screen, rubbing at his eyes.

'Otto, you do know that it's half past four in the morning, don't you?' Nigel moaned.

'Sorry, Nigel but this couldn't wait,' Otto snapped back.

'What?'

'See for yourself.' Otto pointed the camera at the rampaging monster that had once been Nigel's science project.

'Violet!' Nigel cried, and Otto turned the camera back towards himself. 'Oh my God, what's happened to her?'

'I was hoping that you might be able to tell us, Nigel,' Otto replied, trying to keep his voice calm.

'She was fine last night. I checked on her before I came back to my quarters. I have no idea what could have caused this.'

Otto looked down at the scene below. The squirming mass of lethal-looking tendrils had now covered the entire floor of the cavern. As he watched he was horrified to see a mass of these tendrils rip the cover from a ventilation shaft that was set into the cavern wall and fling it to one side, more tendrils swarming into the now exposed shaft at a ferocious speed.

'How do we kill it, Nigel?' Otto demanded.

'You can't kill her! She doesn't know what she's doing!' Nigel wailed.

'It's her or us, Nigel. If we don't stop her she's going to

overrun the entire school. So how do we kill her?' Otto was losing his patience.

Nigel hesitated for a second, a look of tortured indecision on his face. 'There's a bundle of nerve clusters at the base of her stem. You have to destroy those to kill her.'

Otto peered down into the cavern trying to pick out anything at the base of the monstrous stem. Then he saw them – pulsating slime-covered sacs arranged in a circle around the stem, each one the size of a small car.

'OK, I see them.'

'I've got to come down there. Perhaps I can calm her down,' Nigel said frantically.

The monster's huge head tipped back and let out another screeching roar like fingernails being dragged down a blackboard.

'I think it might be a bit late for that Nigel. Stay where you are.'

The chief of security ran up to Nero as Otto flipped the Blackbox shut.

'It's in the shafts, sir. At the rate that thing's growing it'll overrun the whole school in a couple of hours.' He didn't appear to have an immediate suggestion as to what they could do about it. Behind the chief, security guards fanned out along the walkway. Some were carrying flamethrowers with large fuel tanks strapped to their backs and others were armed with shoulder-mounted rocket launchers.

'Very well, Chief. Hit it with everything you've got. Let's see how much damage this thing can withstand,' Nero instructed.

'Make sure they aim for those growths at the base of the stem,' Otto added, relaying Nigel's advice.

The chief nodded and yelled instructions to his men, who were now spread out along the length of the walkway, before shouting, 'Fire at will!'

The guards did not need to be told twice, and multiple rockets streaked down from the walkway towards the creature below. The tendrils surrounding the base of the creature reacted impossibly fast, springing into the air and swatting the warheads aside before any of them could find their mark, the missiles exploding harmlessly against the walls or in the masses of squirming tentacles. There was no way the guards could destroy the nerve clusters from their current position. Round after round was swatted away before they got anywhere near finding their mark. Nero looked even more worried than before.

'Chief, lock down the accommodation blocks. If that thing reaches the students we'll have a massacre on our hands.'

☢☢☢

In accommodation area seven Laura and Shelby sat dejectedly on one of the sofas in the atrium. Neither of them felt like talking about the disastrous failure of their escape attempt, but at the same time both of them were much too wired to sleep. Suddenly from all around them there came thumping clangs.

'What's that?' Laura shouted over the noise.

Shelby looked around the atrium as the noise continued. 'They're sealing the ventilation shafts,' she replied as yet more steel sheets slid into place behind the grille dotted around the accommodation block's walls.

'They don't seriously think we're going to go crawling around in there again tonight, do they?' Laura moaned. 'We get the message!' she shouted at their unseen tormentors.

'I think they know that,' Shelby answered softly as the noise stopped. A grinding noise from behind them caught their attention and they both turned to see a huge metal slab closing off the entrance to the block. Shelby looked across to the other entrance way at the far end of the cavern. That too was being sealed shut.

'I don't think they're trying to keep us in.' She looked carefully at Laura. 'I think they're trying to keep something out.'

☻☻☻

Meanwhile in the hydroponics cavern, the tendrils were climbing the walls and it was all the guards could do to drive them back from their previously safe perch.

'We're out of ammo for the launchers, sir. I'm running out of ideas here,' the chief said, anxiously eyeing the tendrils that were climbing the walls towards them.

'Get as many of the helicopters ready for take-off as possible,' Nero instructed. He knew that it would be impossible to get everyone off the island that way but he might be able to save at least some of the students.

'Yes, sir.' The chief jogged away and began to issue more frantic orders to his men.

Otto looked around the cavern, trying not to look at the terrifying mass of swarming thorn-covered vines below. He glanced up at the ceiling. His eyes widened.

He turned to Dr Nero. 'Dr Nero, I may have an idea.' He briefly explained what he was proposing to Nero, whose expression changed from one of doubt to one of intense calculation.

'Under any other circumstances I would say you were insane, Malpense, but that might work,' Nero said with a grim smile just as Raven ran out on to the walkway. There was not much that surprised his most capable operative, but Nero saw the look of astonishment on her face as she took in the scene in the cavern below.

'Raven,' Nero shouted over the sounds of the guards firing at the creature, 'over here.' She seemed reluctant to tear her eyes from the monstrous plant as she approached Nero.

'We never have small problems, do we, Max?' she said in a quiet voice.

'This one is bigger than most, I fear,' he replied, his face grave.

He quickly explained the plan that Otto had proposed to him a moment earlier.

'I get all the fun jobs, don't I?' she said, giving Nero a predatory grin.

'Go with Malpense to collect the items he needs, I'm sure I don't have to tell you to hurry. And keep an eye on him, we wouldn't want him to slip away in the confusion, would we?'

'We'll be back before you even notice we're gone,' she replied, turning to Otto.

Wing eyed the black-clad woman warily. 'What did you get yourself into now, Otto?'

'I'm not sure,' Otto replied, 'but I'm not going to argue with her, are you?'

'I should come with you. I don't trust that woman.'

'Neither do I, Wing, but you're hurt. You should stay here.' Wing was still holding his wrist carefully. If anything did happen Otto knew that Wing would not be able to help very much with a broken wrist. Besides, the creature had probably spread throughout H.I.V.E. by now and there was no point them both ending up as fertilizer if something went wrong.

'Malpense! You're with me.' Raven's tone made it clear that she was not prepared to discuss the situation.

☢☢☢

Several dozen students had now gathered in the atrium of accommodation area seven, woken by the sounds of distant explosions and nervously discussing what was going on outside the firmly sealed block. Laura looked over at the heavy steel doors as another explosion made the atrium floor shudder.

'I wish I knew what was going on,' she said, turning to Shelby. 'You don't think it's got anything to do with Otto and Wing, do you?'

There was the sound of distant gunfire. 'I hope not,' Shelby replied, 'for their sake.'

Laura saw a frightened-looking Nigel making his way through the gathering crowd towards them.

'Hey, Nigel. You having trouble sleeping too?' Shelby asked as he approached.

'Erm . . . yes . . . look, there's something you should know.'

It took Nigel a couple of minutes to hurriedly explain the disaster that was unfolding at that very moment in the hydroponics cavern. The two girls stared at him in amazement.

'Well I've heard of people trying to live up to their family name, Nigel, but it sounds like you've really outdone yourself,' Shelby said with a grim smile. 'So we're all on the menu for Frankenflower. Great, just when I thought tonight couldn't get any better.'

'I don't understand what happened,' Nigel said sadly. 'Violet was so small, I just don't see how –'

He was interrupted by a scream from elsewhere in the atrium. They all turned to see what the commotion was and saw several people pointing up towards the ceiling. Laura looked up and saw dozens of thick green vines swarming out of the cave from which the atrium's waterfall flowed, squirming across the rock and quickly advancing down the cascade towards the floor. No one had to tell the assembled students what to do – almost as one they seemed to turn and run for the lifts at the other end of the atrium.

'This way,' Shelby said, steering Laura and Nigel away from the crowd forming around the lifts and towards the stairs. Shelby bounded up the stairs three at a time with Laura and Nigel following close behind.

They came out on to the walkway that led to their own quarters and looked down into the atrium. The doors of the lift carrying the last load of students slid shut moments before the slithering vines reached them, whisking the terrified students upwards to temporary safety. The thorn-covered tendrils slammed against the glass of the elevator shaft, trying to find a way in.

'We're locked in with that thing,' Laura said as they watched the writhing green mass below expanding to cover more and more of the atrium floor. 'There's a limit to how far we can run. We have to try to find a way to stop it.'

With a crash, the glass on one side of one of the lift shafts gave way and the vines crawled inside.

'I'm open to suggestions,' Shelby replied grimly.

⊛⊛⊛

Otto had trouble keeping up with Raven as they ran down the corridor towards the Tactical Education department. They had passed a couple of squads of security guards hurrying to other areas of the facility but otherwise the corridors were eerily deserted. Otto tried to ignore the noises that were coming from the ventilation grilles that they passed, but it was clear that the creature was expanding throughout H.I.V.E. at a alarming rate.

They rounded a corner and came to the entrance to the grappler cavern. Raven quickly punched a code into the panel beside the doors and they slid apart, granting them access. Otto dashed to the racks of grapplers and hurriedly shoved two into his backpack. Raven scanned the cavern impatiently. There was no sign of the creature anywhere but she was not about to let her guard down.

'OK,' Otto said, turning to Raven, 'next stop the Tech department, but we need to find a weapon locker.'

'There are several on the way,' Raven replied as they hurried out of the cavern. 'Are you sure you can make the required modifications?'

'I hope so,' Otto didn't sound entirely certain, 'but I'll need some of the tools in the Tech labs.'

'The creature has been sighted in that area, we should proceed with caution.' Raven set off down the corridor at the same breakneck pace as before. Once again Otto struggled to keep up with her. If they did encounter the creature, being a slow runner would not be a good thing.

☢☢☢

On the walkway overlooking the hydroponics cavern the situation was quickly becoming desperate.

'The flame units are low on fuel, sir,' the chief informed Nero, trying to keep his voice steady, 'I don't know how much longer we can hold the walkway.'

'We have to hold it chief, at least until Raven and the boy return,' Nero replied. 'Do everything you can.'

'Yes, sir.' The chief hurried over to his men and redeployed the few flamethrowers that remained functional along the length of the walkway. Nero knew that the situation was desperate, but they had to hold this position to give Malpense's plan any chance of working.

Without warning a huge tendril reared up into the air above the walkway. It was as thick as a tree trunk and covered in vicious-looking thorns. The guard nearest to the whipping tentacle fired his flamethrower straight at it with little effect. The tendril recoiled momentarily before lashing out and slamming the guard violently against the rock wall. It continued to thrash around the walkway, looking for new prey.

Wing backed away from the flailing tentacle. There was no cover on the walkway and as his back pressed against the rough rock wall he realised that there was nowhere to run. Suddenly the tentacle, seeming to sense his presence, whipped towards him at blinding speed.

'Fanchu, get down!' Nero yelled, sprinting towards the boy. Knowing it was pointless, Wing raised his one good arm to defend himself as the creature prepared to strike. Nero hit Wing hard, pushing him to one side as the tendril hit, the savage thorns raking across the older man's chest and throwing him several metres along the platform. Wing gasped in pain as he landed on his injured wrist, spots swimming before his eyes. Several of the guards hurried down the walkway and used the last few precious kilos of fuel in their flamethrowers to drive the monstrous tendril back before it could strike again. Wing struggled to his feet and limped towards Nero's crumpled body. As he knelt next to the Doctor he was relieved to see that, while his chest rose and fell irregularly, the man was at least still breathing.

Wing carefully rolled Nero on to his back. There was a lot of blood, his shirt had been torn open and several long deep gashes gaped across his chest. A glint caught Wing's eye and, as he looked closer, his mouth dropped open in astonishment. Nero was wearing an amulet that was the perfect mirror image of his own, the yin to his own yang. Wing's mind reeled as he touched the amulet. There was no doubt about it – the symbols they both wore were perfect twins.

'Medics!' the chief of security screamed when he saw Nero lying injured on the walkway, and Wing was shoved to one side as several guards and medics swarmed around the unconscious headmaster. 'We have to get him to the infirmary now, he's losing too much blood,' the chief instructed frantically as the medics assembled a portable stretcher next to Nero.

'The infirmary's cut off, sir. That thing is running rampant in the corridors between here and there,' one of the guards quickly reported.

'Do what you can for him here,' the chief instructed. He looked down at the tendrils that were now slithering up the wall towards the walkway. If they didn't stop this thing soon, it wouldn't just be Nero whose survival was in doubt.

☢ ☢ ☢

Otto and Raven had not been able to take the most direct route to the Tech labs. They had found corridors blocked at several points by twisted masses of the deadly green vines and had to find alternate routes. It was fortunate that they both knew the layout of the school like the backs of their hands. Now they were finally near to their destination, and Raven poked her head round the corner, scanning the corridor that led to the lab entrance.

'Looks clear – let's go.' She dashed round the corner and towards the doors, with Otto close behind. Trying to maintain Raven's merciless pace was exhausting.

As they passed through the doors they found that the lab too was deserted. Otto moved around the room gathering the tools he would need as Raven watched the corridor outside nervously.

'I'll need five minutes,' Otto said, pulling from his backpack the sleepers they had collected on the way to the lab.

'You've got three. Hurry,' Raven replied. She could hear the unmistakable slimy rustling sound of the creature's tendrils moving somewhere nearby.

'It's a good job I work well under pressure,' Otto muttered to himself as he set about removing the casings from the Sleepers. He stared at the exposed mechanism. The design was more complex than he had anticipated. He picked up one of the tools he had gathered and set to work as quickly as he could.

☻☻☻

In accommodation area seven the situation was rapidly becoming critical. All of the students were now either locked in their quarters, trapped by the tendrils or, like Laura, Shelby and Nigel, were crowded on to the upper landing watching with horror as the mutated plant crept slowly upwards towards them.

'How do we stop this thing, Nigel?' Shelby demanded. The tendrils would be on them in a matter of seconds.

'I'm not sure,' Nigel replied desperately. 'Fire would harm her, but we'd probably just end up burning the school down. Besides which, these aren't dry twigs, this is fresh green growth. It'd be very hard to burn.'

'OK, fire's out. What else?' Laura asked.

'Cold. Violet's a tropical plant, she hates the cold,' Nigel said weakly.

If Laura had been a comic-book character, a light bulb would have appeared above her head. She ran to the fire alarm on the wall and smashed the glass with her elbow.

She knew that with H.I.V.E.mind offline the automatic fire suppression system would not kick in, but she also knew from previous discussions with Otto that there was a back-up plan for just such an occasion. All around the landings hatches slid open and fire extinguishers slid from hidden compartments.

'Grab an extinguisher, Shelby,' Laura yelled, taking one for herself. She ran towards a point on the landing where the first few tendrils were starting to appear over the edge of the balcony, and depressed the lever of the fire extinguisher. An icy-white cloud of carbon dioxide gas shot out, enveloping the waving tendrils and making them recoil instantly as if they had been burnt. Shelby also fired her extinguisher at the encroaching tentacles, quickly repelling them from the balcony.

'Brand, you're a genius!' Shelby shouted happily as several other students who had seen what the two girls had done snatched their own extinguishers from the wall.

However, Laura knew that it was a temporary reprieve at best – there were only so many fire extinguishers on the top landing and they would not last for ever.

☁☁☁

Otto snapped the casing back on to the final sleeper and shoved the weapons back into his pack.

'OK, all done. Let's go,' Otto said as he jogged across

the lab towards Raven. She turned towards him and the look on her face sent a chill through him.

'I'm afraid it might be too late,' she said quietly.

Otto looked into the corridor and saw that the only route back to the hydroponics cavern was blocked by a mass of the creature's tendrils. They only had to get a few metres past the seething green barricade but it might as well have been miles away.

'How fast can you run?' Raven asked, never taking her eyes from the approaching vines.

'Fast enough, especially when my life depends on it,' Otto whispered.

'Stay close to me. When I say run, you go and don't look back. Understood?'

Otto nodded.

'I think it's time this thing got a pruning.' Raven reached both hands over her shoulders and drew the twin gleaming swords from their sheaths on her back. She advanced towards the tendrils, her pace calm and measured, Otto just a metre or so behind her. The thorned vines seemed to sense her presence, rearing up from the floor as she approached. Raven kept moving forwards, both swords drawn, waiting for the first inevitable attack. She did not have to wait long – several of the tendrils suddenly whipped towards her and Otto, eager for fresh prey. Raven reacted instantly, both swords swinging in lightning arcs through the air, neatly severing all of the attacking vines, the dead ends dropping to the floor with a wet slapping sound. Raven continued to advance, repelling each strike as it came. The nearer they got to the passage leading to the hydroponics cavern the faster the vines whirled, Raven's swords becoming little more than a silver blur as she hacked a way through. With only a couple of metres to go, one of the dozens of tendrils that were simultaneously attacking snuck past her guard, ripping a long gash into her thigh. Raven grunted in pain but never slowed, swinging the two blades even faster now as she carved a path through the spinning green blizzard for Otto and herself. They were now only a couple of metres from the adjoining corridor, which appeared to be mercifully free of the monstrous vines. Raven slashed to one side, finally clearing the path enough for them to get through.

'Go!' Raven shouted. 'Run as fast as you can! I can't hold them back for ever.' Her face and uniform were streaked with the green juices that sprayed from the severed tendrils, her once gleaming blades dripping with the same foul slime. Otto knew there was no time to argue. He leapt through the gap that Raven had cut and sprinted down the corridor. Several tendrils snaked down the corridor after him.

'You should be worried about me, not him!' Raven

yelled, hacking at the vines with even greater ferocity. The tendrils pursuing Otto seemed to hesitate for a moment before coiling back on themselves and joining the dozens of others slashing at Raven.

Despite Raven's instructions to the contrary, Otto could not help but look back as he ran down the corridor. He could just make out the dark figure amidst the twisting coils of the vines, her blades still flashing, before the green wall thickened and she disappeared finally from view.

☸ ☸ ☸

'That's it! I'm out,' Shelby shouted as she threw the empty fire extinguisher at the approaching tendrils. She and Laura had fought desperately to hold the tendrils back as the last few students had locked themselves in their rooms but it had done little good.

'Open up!' Laura shouted, banging on the last door on the landing. The door slid open slightly and Nigel's terrified face appeared in the gap.

'Are they gone?' He squeaked.

'No, but we will be if you don't let us in,' Laura said angrily.

'OK, OK,' Nigel replied, opening the door fully.

'Come on, Shelby, we've got to get inside!' Laura shouted.

The two girls ran through the door as Nigel shut and locked it behind them.

'Where's Franz?' Shelby asked, looking around the room.

'He locked himself in the bathroom. He won't come out,' Nigel explained.

'And I am being quite happy to stay here,' Franz's muffled voice added from behind the bathroom door.

'We should be safe in here, shouldn't we?' Nigel asked, looking from one girl to the other.

There was an enormous bang from the room's main door and the thick metal buckled inwards slightly.

'Oh, sure, for about the next two minutes,' Shelby replied.

☻☻☻

Otto ran out on to the walkway to find a scene of utter chaos. The tendrils were attacking from all sides now as two guards wielding the last pair of functional flame-throwers fought to keep them at bay. Nero lay propped against the wall, his eyes closed and blood-soaked bandages wrapped around his chest, his face pale. Crouched next to Nero were Wing and the chief, who both looked up in surprise as Otto appeared.

'Otto!' Wing shouted, grinning at him. 'Are you OK? Where's Raven?'

'She didn't make it,' Otto said quietly. 'What happened to Nero?'

'He was wounded when the creature attacked us. We have to get him to the infirmary but the way is blocked by that thing.' Wing jerked his head in the direction of the hideous mutated plant in the middle of the cavern; it had grown noticeably in the time that Otto had been away. 'It should be me lying there instead of him. He was hurt while trying to protect me.' Wing looked distracted – the experience had clearly shaken him.

'It's time to end this,' Otto said, pulling the pair of grapplers from his pack, 'one way or the other.' He snapped the grapplers to his wrists and moved quickly to the railing at the edge of the walkway. The scene that greeted him as he looked down into the base of the cavern was like a vision of hell. Boiling masses of vines surrounded the monstrous head of the creature which strained towards the walkway, desperate to reach the tantalising morsels that lay just beyond its reach. At the rate that it appeared to be growing they would not remain beyond its reach for long.

Otto forced himself to look away from the creature and picked out the points on the cavern ceiling that he needed to reach. The original idea had been for Raven to carry out this stage of the plan but that, sadly, was no longer going to be possible. He tried not to think about the way in which she had sacrificed herself to save him.

He had to stay focused on what he needed to do next. Not even Wing could help Otto now – with his injured wrist there was no way he could use a grappler. He was going to have to do this alone.

'Otto, there's something that I have to tell you about Nero,' Wing said urgently.

'You can tell me when I get back,' Otto said, pointing the grappler on his right arm at the ceiling. Wing stared at him, desperate to tell him what he had seen, but there was no time.

'Good luck,' Wing said softly, placing his hand on Otto's shoulder.

'I don't believe in luck,' Otto said, forcing a smile. He squeezed the trigger, the thin wire shooting upwards and securing itself firmly to the rocky cavern ceiling. He took a long, deep breath and swung out into the cavern.

The creature seemed to sense the sudden movement, its head whipping around towards Otto as he swung through the air. Otto knew that he had to keep the line attaching him to the ceiling a certain length to keep up his momentum. He silently prayed that he would still be beyond the monster's reach. As the creature's head rushed towards him he tried to concentrate on the arcs that his brain was plotting in the air ahead of him. He fired the second grappler, releasing the first bolt as soon as he felt the second line go taut. The creature's bloated head shot after him, only momentarily confused by the slight change in his original trajectory.

Concentrate on where you're going, Otto told himself, and whatever you do don't look down. He maintained the rhythm of his swings, heading towards the centre of the cavern. He couldn't see the creature's head – he knew that it was somewhere behind him, but he had no idea how far away. He switched lines again, just as the slime-covered jaws of the creature slammed shut on the empty air where he had hung a split second before. He reeled the line in slightly, hoping that it would be enough to keep him beyond the reach of the snapping jaws. Just a couple more swings and he'd reach his target. The monster's head raced at him again, moving impossibly fast. Otto twisted desperately, altering his course just enough that the gaping jaws snapped shut on empty air once more. The side of the creature's head hit him hard, setting Otto spinning on the end of the line, momentarily disorienting him. Otto fired blindly towards the centre of the cavern, hoping that the grappler bolt would strike home. He felt the line go taut and swing again, his whole body aching from the glancing blow the monster had dealt him.

Otto fired again and the grappler bolt shot into the forest of hanging stalactites in the centre of the cavern's roof. He reeled in the line, drawing himself up into the massive natural rock formation, beyond the reach of the creature's hungry jaws. He twisted on the end of the line as he rose, taking in the shape of the jagged hanging rocks, looking for the best place to plant the surprise he had in store for the monster below. He spotted a small hollow in the rocks, near to what he calculated must be the most vulnerable point of the formation, and thumbed the controls on the grappler to reel him up towards it. As he rose towards the gap in the rock he caught a glimpse of the distant walkway and was horrified to see that the crawling vines had completely overrun the platform, forcing Wing and the guards to fall back through the doorway and along the corridor that Otto had run down just minutes before. Otto felt a chill run down his spine as he realised that there was no way back along that corridor. Wing was trapped between the vines advancing from the cavern and the ones flooding down the corridor. He pressed the button on the grappler harder, willing the line to reel in faster. He felt as if he was rising agonisingly slowly, but after only a couple of seconds he was level with the crack in the rock.

Dangling from the ceiling by one arm he struggled to pull the sleepers from the pack on his back. He placed the first weapon carefully in the hollow in the rock, praying that his alterations would work as planned. He worked fast, pulling the remaining three sleepers from his bag and placing them side by side in the small hole. He paused for a moment and looked at the four guns lying there. Would it be enough? He forced the question from his mind. If the modification he had made did not work as planned it was too late to do anything about it now. He reached out and pulled the trigger on the first sleeper. Nothing happened. He pulled the trigger again – still nothing. What had he missed? Just as Otto began to panic he heard a slight whining noise which began to gradually increase in volume. It was working! He quickly pulled the triggers on the other three sleepers and thumbed the switch on the grappler which would reel him down. He knew he only had a minute or so to get clear.

Otto caught a flicker of movement out of the corner of his eye and suddenly felt a blinding pain in his ankle. He looked down and saw a thin tendril wrapped around his left foot, its grip still tightening. He gasped in pain as the tendril pulled hard on his leg, dragging him down towards the creature's gaping mouth, just twenty metres below. He locked the grappler holding him to the ceiling, trying to stop his descent towards certain death, the mechanism on the back of the device screeching in protest as the vine continued to pull him inexorably downwards. Otto yelled out in pain – it felt as if he was going to be torn in two. He gritted his teeth and pointed the grappler on his free hand downwards, aiming carefully. If he missed this shot he wouldn't get another. He squeezed the trigger and the silver bolt shot from the grappler, straight at the slimy green tentacle attached to his leg. The bolt went straight through the tendril in an explosion of green slime and he instantly felt it release its grip on his ankle, recoiling back towards the cavern floor. Otto hit the bolt release, praying that the line would not get tangled in the flailing vines below. He watched helplessly as the line reeled in and felt a flood of relief as the bolt snapped back into place on his wrist, its silver tip covered in a thin layer of the creature's emerald blood. Otto fired the grappler again at a distant point on the ceiling. The length of the line would send him swinging dangerously close to the cavern floor, but he knew he had to get as far away from the centre of the cavern as he could.

He released the other grappler and swung downwards at terrifying speed towards the tendril-covered floor below. As he swung low over the writhing green mass, tendrils snaked upwards, reaching for him. A couple got close but he was moving too fast now and they flailed uselessly at the empty air as he rocketed past, now swinging upwards again towards the platform crawling with tentacles.

THOOM!!

Behind Otto all four sleepers overloaded at once. The massive sonic shockwave tore through the hanging forest of stalactites, shattering their centuries-old grip on the cavern ceiling. The creature gave a final thunderous screeching roar as tens of thousands of tons of rock gave in to the pull of gravity and smashed into the floor below, crushing the bloated head and its vulnerable nerve sacs to pulp, burying the monster for ever.

The shockwave hit Otto in the back like a charging rhino, knocking the wind from him and snapping his grappler line. He seemed to fly through the air for a moment before he smashed into the suspended walkway with a bone-crunching impact. Stunned, Otto lay on the walkway, amidst the twitching tendrils, harmless now that the creature was dead. He rolled over and forced himself up into a sitting position, surveying the enormous mountain of rubble that filled the centre of the cavern, now partially obscured by the thick clouds of dust that hung in the air.

'You're compost, pal,' he muttered to himself, chuckling despite the pain in his ribs. As he struggled to his feet his whole body protested. The adrenaline rush he had been feeling ebbed away to be replaced by fresh aches. His whole body felt like one big bruise.

Suddenly the platform lurched beneath his feet. The shockwave had not only loosened the huge stalactites' grip on the ceiling, it had also loosened the fixings that secured the walkway to the wall. With a screech of tearing metal the walkway began to collapse. Otto ran for the doorway in the rock wall, every muscle protesting.

He was only a couple of metres from safety when the whole walkway collapsed, tearing away from the wall with a horrendous screeching noise.

Otto dived forwards as the floor fell away beneath his feet. He slammed into the edge of the corridor, dangling over the lethal drop to the cavern floor, his feet scrabbling for purchase on the rough rock wall. It was no good – he slipped and fell, just catching the edge of the walkway with his fingertips. He tried desperately to pull himself up, but the toll that the past few hours had taken on his body was too great – he felt his tenuous grip slipping. He closed his eyes. He wasn't scared, just angry that he had made it this far only to fail at the end. Just as he felt that finally, inevitably, he was going to fall, a hand closed on his wrist, its grip like iron. He looked upwards.

'You don't get rid of me that easily, kid.' Raven's face, streaked with the creature's green blood, smiled back down at him.

Chapter 16

Laura slowly opened her eyes. The tendrils that had smashed through the door just seconds before lay convulsing harmlessly on the floor. She looked across the room at Nigel and Shelby, their own expressions of astonishment matching her own. Stepping cautiously over the fallen tendrils, she poked her head through the ruined doorway. All over the cavern the tendrils lay motionless, giving no hint of their previous murderous intent. Shelby and Nigel followed her out on to the balcony, gaping in disbelief at the piles of dead vines.

'What happened?' Shelby said quietly as more doors began to hiss open around the cavern.

'Divine intervention?' Laura replied.

'They must have destroyed the nerve clusters,' Nigel said quietly.

'Oh, who cares,' Shelby grinned, 'as long as we don't have to clear it up.'

They headed off down the balcony towards the stairs, picking their way through the dead vines.

Back in the room a small voice came from behind the bathroom door.

'Hello? Hello? Is anybody being there?'

☻☻☻

'Max . . . Max, can you hear me?' Raven gently stroked Nero's cheek. He was still worryingly pale. His eyes flickered open.

'Natalya,' he whispered, his voice croaky. 'The school?'

'It's over, Max. The creature is dead and the school is safe.' She smiled. 'I think we might need a new hydroponics facility, though.'

'Well done. I knew you could do it,' Nero replied with a smile.

'Actually, it wasn't me, I was . . . occupied elsewhere. It was Malpense. He carried out the plan himself. It worked, Max.'

'Malpense?' Nero's surprise was obvious. 'Where is he? I want to thank him.'

'I'll get him for you, he's just over there . . .' Raven's voice trailed off.

'What is it, Natalya?' Nero asked urgently.

Otto and Wing were gone.

☻☻☻

Otto and Wing ran across the gantry towards the helicopter sitting ready on the crater landing pad. Otto had heard Nero give the emergency evacuation orders and had hoped that it would mean that the way to the landing pad was clear. Just as he'd expected, there were no guards anywhere to be seen. They were too busy dealing with the chaos elsewhere in the school. He looked upwards. The crater was open and for the first time in months he saw clear blue sky. It was a strangely moving sight.

Suddenly Wing slowed, coming to a halt halfway across the gantry, still clutching his injured wrist.

'Come on, Wing, this is our chance. I can fly that thing, trust me.'

'Otto,' Wing replied, looking down at the floor, 'I can't leave.'

Otto stared at his friend in amazement.

'What do you mean, you can't leave? What was last night about? This could be our only chance.' Otto didn't understand. What had happened to Wing?

'I tried to tell you earlier. It's Nero.'

'What about him?' Otto was getting annoyed – they didn't have time for this.

'When he was injured I saw something. He was wearing the other half of my mother's amulet.'

Otto suddenly understood Wing's tortured expression. 'I thought you said it was lost?' he said quietly.

'It was, until today. I have to know where he got it from . . . I have to know if he took it from my mother.'

'Wing, I understand, I really do, but this might be our only chance to get off this rock. Is it really that important to you?'

Wing looked up at Otto, his eyes filled with sadness. 'Yes . . . it is. I cannot leave.'

Otto felt his anger flare. 'Fine. You can stay here because of a piece of jewellery if you want, but I'm leaving.' He started walking towards the helicopter.

'Otto, please, I need your help. You have been a great friend to me and I am not sure I can survive here alone. I know I can defend myself physically, but mentally, I just don't have your strength. Without you I fear that the darkness in this place will consume me.'

Otto stopped, his hand on the helicopter door handle. He had never had a friend like Wing before. Always too busy trying to outwit everyone around him, he'd never had the time or the inclination to worry about his own loneliness. But something inside him had changed. Wing had risked his life for him without hesitation, and now Otto was going to repay him by just abandoning him here. He thought about Laura and Shelby, how he had promised them that he would get them out of here, away from H.I.V.E. Could he just leave them all behind? He heard Nero's words from earlier that day echoing in his mind.

'Where exactly did you think you were going?' Otto whispered to himself.

He took his hand from the door handle and turned to face Wing, a half smile on his face.

'We're going to have to do something about that snoring.'

☢☢☢

Nero sat at his desk surveying the latest damage reports. It had taken several weeks to clear the school of the remains of Nigel Darkdoom's mutated science project and his engineers had informed him that the new hydroponics dome would take months to complete. The chief had also told him that six of his guards had lost their lives in the battle against the creature and Nero had given him strict instructions that their dependents, if they had any, were to be discreetly given any support that H.I.V.E. could offer. Miraculously none of the students had been seriously injured. There were a couple of broken bones, some cuts and bruises, but nothing more. It could have been much worse.

Normally he would have punished the four students who had attempted to escape, but given their heroism during the crisis he had taken no action against them. Malpense in particular had shown unusual courage. There was no doubt that the boy showed extraordinary potential, if they could actually manage to keep him on the island for the next six years. Nero had summoned

Malpense to his office shortly after the crisis and had thanked him for his extraordinary efforts to save the school. He'd also told him that he didn't want to hear about any more escape plans being made.

Malpense had looked him straight in the eye and said, 'Don't worry, Doctor. You won't hear about them.'

Nero had also given strict instructions that no one who knew what had happened was to discuss Nigel Darkdoom's part in creating the monster that had so nearly destroyed the school. A couple of members of staff and the chief of security had requested that the boy be expelled for his part in the disaster but Nero had dismissed their demands. If anything, it showed that the Darkdoom boy had a great deal of untapped potential – indeed, in the right circumstances the creature he had created might even have been useful. The boy had more of his father in him than he realised.

At precisely the appointed time the video screen on the wall flickered into life. Number One sat hidden in shadow as usual. Nero had not spoken to him since the crisis and, while he had submitted reports on the incident to their anonymous leader, he was not sure what Number One's reaction would be. Nero had not been looking forward to the conversation.

'Good morning, Maximilian. You have had an interesting couple of weeks, I see,' the shadowy figure said.

'Yes, sir. It was a regrettable incident, but the school is now virtually returned to normal.'

'So I see from your status reports. I also see that the Malpense boy should take most of the credit for defusing the situation.'

Nero knew that the reports he had sent were largely accurate, but he doubted that Number One knew just how close they had come to total disaster.

'Yes sir, he showed remarkable initiative.'

'Just as he did during his escape attempt, I note. Do you think he may become a problem?'

'No, sir. I am quite used to dealing with the more . . . *precocious* students, as you know.'

'Indeed. I'm sure I do not need to remind you of the consequences if you were to let the boy slip through your fingers.'

'No, sir. I understand.'

'Good. Be thankful that he was not seriously injured during the events of that day, Nero. If Malpense is killed he will not be making the journey into the next life unaccompanied.'

'Yes, sir. It is difficult to provide him with constant protection discreetly, but we will of course continue to do our best.'

'I am not interested in your best, Nero. He is to remain unharmed, no excuses.'

'Understood.'

'Good. Will you require any extra resources to assist in the reconstruction of the damaged areas of the facility?'

'No, Number One, I believe we have everything in hand.'

'Very well. You will be attending the G.L.O.V.E. command meeting in Vienna next month.' It was not a question.

'Yes sir, I had received notification.'

'This will be an important meeting, Nero. I have something critical to discuss with the assembled commanders.'

'I look forward to it,' Nero lied.

'I'm sure you do, Maximilian. That will be all.'

The screen went dark and Nero let out a long sigh of relief. Number One was notoriously unpredictable – too many men had thought they had pleased him only to find that their next appointment was with a remarkably well-stocked piranha tank. The fact that he himself was still breathing suggested that he had not lost his superior's confidence. Nero knew that if Malpense had ended up as a snack for Darkdoom's rampaging creation he might as well have jumped down the creature's throat after him. He didn't like being kept in the dark about something upon which his life so obviously depended. He had to find out more about the boy, and he had to do it fast.

297

Number One watched as Nero's calm face disappeared from his own video screen. Nero had always been good at concealing his nervousness, but Number One knew that H.I.V.E.'s headmaster was unsure of his own fate given the fiasco that had taken place at the school. He should be worried – Number One was not tolerant of mistakes, even from his most trusted operatives. Fear was a remarkably effective tool and G.L.O.V.E.'s commander knew precisely how best to wield it.

He sat back in his chair, a smile on his face. Nero was a ruthless and devious man, but he had weaknesses, his love for his school being primary amongst them. Those who knew his prior history would be astonished at the care with which Nero protected H.I.V.E. and its students. It was rather like one of those sickeningly saccharine news stories of some dangerous wild predator looking after a litter of orphaned kittens.

Given this protectiveness, he knew he had to proceed carefully. He was not sure if he could depend on Nero's loyalty if the man ever found out exactly what Number One actually had in mind for the Malpense boy. He smiled again as he thought through what he had planned for the boy's future. One day Nero and the boy would discover exactly what this plan was – indeed, it was essential that they did – and on that day Otto Malpense would wish he'd never been born.